"I'd love to show you how a real Marine woos a woman."

Joe leaned closer. "After I take care of my duty and give the Sergeant Major's kid her tour. So which one is she? The one with the pigtails?"

"No." Prudence was silent.

"Then she must be the one with the glasses."

"Wrong again," Prudence said coolly.

Joe frowned. "But he told me his daughter's class was here for a tour."

"His daughter's class *is* here for a tour."

Joe had a bad feeling. "You mean…?"

"That I'm the Sergeant Major's daughter?" the sexy teacher said with a smug smile. "Yes, that's exactly what I mean."

* * *

Praise for Cathie's previous title

Daddy in Dress Blues (SR #1470)

"Funny, sweet—I couldn't put it down!
One of Cathie Linz's best books. Imagine a
hard-core Marine trying to raise a three-year-old
daughter by the Marine Corps training manual!
Doesn't that just about say it all?"
—*New York Times* bestselling author
Susan Elizabeth Phillips

Dear Reader,

I'm dreaming of summer vacations—of sitting by the beach, dangling my feet in a lake, walking on a mountain or curling up in a hammock. And in each vision, I have a Silhouette Romance novel, and I'm happy. Why don't you grab a couple and join me? And in each book take a look at our Silhouette Makes You a Star contest!

We've got some terrific titles in store for you this month. Longtime favorite author Cathie Linz has developed some delightful stories with U.S. Marine heroes and *Stranded with the Sergeant* is appealing and fun. Cara Colter has the second of her THE WEDDING LEGACY titles for you. *The Heiress Takes a Husband* features a rich young woman who's struggling to prove herself—and the handsome attorney who lends a hand.

Arlene James has written over fifty titles for Silhouette Books, and her expertise shows. *So Dear to My Heart* is a tender, original story of a woman finding happiness again. And Karen Rose Smith—another popular veteran—brings us *Doctor in Demand*, about a wounded man who's healed by the love of a woman and her child.

And two newer authors round out the list! Melissa McClone's *His Band of Gold* is an emotional realization of the power of love, and Sue Swift debuts in Silhouette Romance with *His Baby, Her Heart*, in which a woman agrees to fulfill her late sister's dream of children. It's an unusual and powerful story that is part of our THE BABY'S SECRET series.

Enjoy these stories, and make time to appreciate yourselves in your hectic lives! Have a wonderful summer.

Happy reading!

Mary-Theresa Hussey

Mary-Theresa Hussey
Senior Editor

Please address questions and book requests to:
Silhouette Reader Service
U.S.: 3010 Walden Ave., P.O. Box 1325, Buffalo, NY 14269
Canadian: P.O. Box 609, Fort Erie, Ont. L2A 5X3

Stranded with the Sergeant

CATHIE LINZ

SILHOUETTE *Romance*

Published by Silhouette Books

America's Publisher of Contemporary Romance

For my "editor extraordinaire," Jennifer Walsh, for loving
my books and bragging about me. I hope we can work
together on the next 40 books! And to all the readers
who've bought my last 40 books, this one is for you!

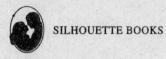 SILHOUETTE BOOKS

ISBN 0-373-19534-6

STRANDED WITH THE SERGEANT

Copyright © 2001 by Cathie L. Baumgardner

This edition published by arrangement with Harlequin Books S.A.

Visit Silhouette at www.eHarlequin.com

Printed in U.S.A.

CATHIE LINZ

left her career in a university law library to become a *USA Today* bestselling author of contemporary romances. She is the recipient of the highly coveted Storyteller of the Year Award given by *Romantic Times Magazine* and was recently nominated for a Love and Laughter Career Achievement Award for the delightful humor in her books.

Cathie enjoys spending time with her family, her two cats, her trusty word processor and her hidden cache of Oreo cookies!

Dear Reader,

I first met Joe Wilder while writing *Daddy in Dress Blues* (SR #1470), where he was the hero's best friend. I knew Joe had to have a book of his own—he told me so himself many times. I also knew that Joe had some dark secrets up his sleeve. Since *I* wanted to know what they were, I sat down to write Joe's story.

A U.S. Marine like Joe, a hunk who could give Mel Gibson a run for his money, needs a very special heroine. I got her name first. Prudence. Yes, a bad boy like Joe would need a prudent woman, one who wouldn't melt at his first sexy smile, one who could see past his charm to the tortured soul inside.

Prudence has secrets, too. She knows what it is like to be consumed with guilt, so she wants to help Joe. But help isn't something a U.S. Marine accepts easily, especially not from his commanding officer's daughter!

I've loved writing about these heroic men who abide by the Marine Corps values of honor, courage and commitment. Come on, admit it—there's just something special about a man in a U.S. Marine dress blues uniform! I hope you enjoy Joe and Prudence's story and watch for more stories from me about these men of honor.

I enjoy hearing from my readers, so please visit my Web site at www.comet.net/writers/linz.

All the best,

Cathie Linz

Chapter One

"So, Wilder, I hear you jumped off another bridge this weekend." Joe Wilder's commanding officer pinned him with a steely-eyed glare. In his late forties, his military haircut tipped with gray, Sergeant Major Richard Martin had a drill instructor's voice and a warrior's demeanor. He reminded Joe of his own father.

"Actually I bungee-jumped, sir," Joe corrected him with the utmost respect, trying to ignore the way the North Carolina sun bounced off the bright white walls of the Sergeant Major's office. The glare made his head pound. He'd woken at 0600 hours with the mother of all hangovers. Joe knew he was in bad shape when merely looking at white wall paint made his head hurt. "I was attached to the structure with a cord."

"I don't care if you were attached to the structure with superglue," Sergeant Major Martin growled. "You still jumped off. And I don't approve. The

United States Marine Corps has spent a lot of time and money on your training, Wilder. I'd hate to see it all wasted with you splattered on a slab of concrete or some rocky riverbed somewhere. Is that understood?''

"Yes, sir."

"If you like jumping out off things that much, you should become a paratrooper."

"Understood, sir."

"I certainly hope so, Wilder." Sergeant Major Martin tapped the folder on his desk impatiently. The sound was amplified tenfold by Joe's hangover, but he showed no outward sign of his discomfort. A Marine never showed signs of discomfort. Honor, courage, commitment. These were the Marine Corps values. Not discomfort. Not guilt.

"Since you've been under my command your off-duty antics have gotten wilder and wilder," Sergeant Major Martin continued. "Why is that?"

Because the risk-taking made Joe feel alive. That's why he did it. To get away from the ever-present nightmares that seemed to be eating him up inside, to escape from the pain and the guilt.

Not that he'd ever tell Sergeant Major Martin that. Not that he'd tell *anyone* that. Everyone thought Joe was just a wild thrill-seeker. Wilder. It wasn't just his name, it had become his attitude.

Which was fine by him. But apparently not fine by his commanding officer. "Your aforementioned wild behavior stops as of right now," the older man ordered in a clipped voice.

"Yes, sir."

"You'll be turning over a new leaf. Starting immediately. I'd like you to escort my daughter's sixth-grade class for a tour of the base here."

Joe blinked, certain he couldn't have heard correctly. "Sir?"

"You heard me."

"I am not that familiar with the base yet, sir," Joe felt compelled to say. He'd only recently been assigned here to Camp Lejeune in coastal North Carolina after completing an overseas deployment he'd rather not think about. Ever. "I'm not sure I'm qualified to give a tour."

"*I* think you're qualified, Wilder, and that's all that matters. I did plan on having Sergeant Brown do the honors, but he had to have emergency surgery last night on a ruptured appendix. So you'll be taking his place."

"Yes, sir."

"And after you give them the tour, you'll be going with them this afternoon on a weekend field trip up into the mountains."

"A field trip, sir?"

"That's right, Wilder. Why the look? Surely after your Marine training, not to mention your love of extreme sport activities, you're not telling me you're afraid of a bunch of kids?"

"No, sir." That much was true. Afraid didn't even come close to the feelings churning in Joe's gut. Panic would be a much more accurate description.

"Glad to hear it. The class is waiting for you down the hall in conference room 1013. Once you've completed the tour, you'll have one hour to gather the necessary equipment, sleeping bag, etc., that you'll need for a weekend camping trip. The route is already laid out for you, following the Sunshine Trailhead in the Blue Ridge Mountains. A three- or four-hour drive to the other side of the state. Here."

Joe willed his hand not to shake as he reached out to take the topographical hiking map.

"My daughter, Prudence, is my little princess, my only child. So I don't want anything ruining this field trip for her. Do you have any questions, Wilder?"

Thousands of them. Why me? Why now? But he bolted those questions down and instead said, "No, sir."

"Good. Glad to hear it. Get a move on then. They're waiting for you, Wilder. Dismissed."

Kids. Why did it have to be kids? Joe stared at his pale reflection in the men's bathroom mirror.

It was only one weekend. Surely he could handle one weekend. He'd handled worse things. He'd... survived.

Joe rubbed the ache between his eyes before reaching into his pocket for the two aspirins he'd meant to take before seeing his commanding officer. He felt like a wimp for taking the analgesic, but he needed to dump this headache so that he could think of a way to dump this assignment.

Of course there was no way he'd refuse an order from his commanding officer. He was a Marine through and through. He'd never willingly be derelict in his duties.

What about that day two months ago? a little voice in his head said. *If you'd done your duty two months ago and gotten on that helicopter, another man wouldn't have died in your place.*

Gritting his teeth, Joe willed the memories away. He needed to keep his act together here. One step at a time. First he'd locate his commanding officer's daughter.

The walk down the hallway from the men's room to the conference room was one of the longest he'd ever taken. To his relief there was another adult in the room. A woman. A good-looking woman. The teacher.

Ignoring all the sixth-graders, he focused his attention on her. Dark brown shoulder-length hair, chocolate-brown eyes, lush mouth, good figure showed off in a pair of well-fitting if conservative khaki pants and white T-shirt. She had a colorful scarf jauntily tied around her neck. She looked to be in her mid-to-late twenties. And she was definitely attractive.

Joe's panic lessened. Here was one area where he still felt like a pro—the male/female arena. This was something he still excelled at, charming women. Flirting was second nature to him.

It started with his smile. He watched her reaction to it. Surprise and appreciation flashed in her dark eyes. Not for long, but long enough for him to catch it.

"Sorry I'm late, ma'am." He added a touch of remorse to his expression.

"And you are?"

"Sergeant Wilder. Sergeant Joe Wilder at your service, ma'am. Before we begin our tour, I've got a question." He drew the teacher aside to a quieter corner. "Which one is she?"

The sexy teacher gave him a blank look. "Excuse me?"

"Which one is Sergeant Major Martin's daughter?"

"Why do you want to know?" She sounded curious.

"Because I've been ordered to give her the deluxe tour of the base and I want to be nice to her."

"I don't think you should single her out for any special treatment."

"Hey, I'm just following orders here."

"Right. *Semper fi.* A Marine always does his duty." Her voice held a new edge.

"You don't sound very pleased about that. I wonder why? Did you date a Marine or something?"

"That's a safe bet," she retorted. "Since this base is home to the largest concentration of Marines and sailors in the world, it would be hard to avoid bumping into a Marine in this part of North Carolina."

"I wouldn't mind bumping into you," Joe murmured with a lopsided grin. "Just name the time and place."

"I no longer date Marines," she loftily informed him.

"Why's that?"

"My reasons are too lengthy to go into here."

"I've got time." He was certainly in no hurry to have to deal with the kids.

"Well, I don't," she replied in irritation. The way she tossed her head and flicked her hair away from her face reminded him of a feral cat he'd tamed as a kid. That cat had refused to let anyone touch it, but Joe had slowly and patiently won it over. That same patience had come in handy where women were concerned.

"So tell me later."

"Why should I do that?" she said.

"Because I'm a nice guy?"

"Who thinks he's God's gift to women."

Ouch. So the little cat had claws. Placing his open hand on his chest, he said, "You wound me, ma'am."

"I sincerely doubt that, Sergeant. I sincerely doubt any woman has wounded you."

"Why? Because I'm a big, tough Marine?"

"Because you use your charm to keep them at a distance."

"Hey, if I'm using my charm to keep women at a distance, then something is definitely wrong with my game plan."

"Game plan? Don't you mean your battle plan?"

"As in battle between the sexes?" Joe moved closer, so that he could smell her perfume. It was tart and citrusy.

Shifting his attention to that lush smart-talking mouth of hers, he wondered if she'd taste as good as she smelled. Oh, yeah, he had no doubt she'd taste better than a cold beer after a long hike.

He had to grin at his own lack of poetry. Beer and a long hike…that sounded like something his best friend Curt Blackwell would say about his new wife, Jessie.

Joe and Curt had gone to boot camp together and been buddies ever since. Curt was a brooding loner, but that didn't seem to stop the ladies from lining up for him. Still, Curt had come to Joe for advice when it mattered, when he'd been reunited with Jessie after years apart.

Joe's advice was good. Jessie had apparently agreed, because she'd become Curt's wife last year in a full Marine dress wedding with Joe there as Curt's best man.

Yeah, this male/female flirting stuff was something Joe could still handle with one arm tied behind his back…although he'd have preferred having one arm around the sexy schoolteacher's shoulders.

She was narrowing her chocolate-brown eyes at him, as if she were able to read his thoughts and wanted to challenge him on their accuracy. Great. He loved a challenge. Especially one that involved a good-looking woman.

"I take it you consider yourself to be an expert in the battle between the sexes," she said.

"My motto is make love, not war."

"I'm sure that didn't come out of the U.S. Marine Procedural Manual."

"If you've been dating guys who base their romantic approach on the Marine Procedural Manual, then I can understand your dissatisfaction," he murmured. "And I'd love to have the chance to show you how a real Marine woos a woman." He leaned closer as if tempting her to kiss him, before leaning away to smile at the startled awareness in her eyes. "After I take care of my duty and give the Sergeant Major's kid her tour. Which one is she? The one with the pigtails and strange socks?"

"No."

He scanned the roomful of kids, trying to look for some kind of familial resemblance. "Then she must be the one with the short haircut and glasses."

"Wrong again," she said coolly.

"Are we going to play twenty questions all day or are you going to tell me which kid is the Sergeant Major's?"

"A few minutes ago you told me you had plenty of time."

"A few minutes ago I did have time until…"

"You wasted it flirting with me?" she countered mockingly.

"Look, cut me some slack here, would you?" he said in exasperation. "I'm having a bad day. Just tell me which kid is the Sergeant Major's so I can figure out where to go from here with this tour stuff. I'm only following…''

"Orders," she completed the sentence for him. "Yes, I heard you the first time you said that."

"So what's the problem?" Joe demanded.

"The problem is that none of these children are Sergeant Major Martin's."

Joe frowned. "But that's not possible. He told me his daughter's class was here for a tour."

"His daughter's class *is* here for a tour."

Joe had a bad feeling. "You mean…?"

"That I'm Sergeant Major Martin's daughter?" the sexy teacher said with a smug smile that didn't bode well for him. "Yes, that's exactly what I mean."

Chapter Two

Prudence Martin watched chagrin flash across Joe Wilder's handsome face. She'd never seen eyes so Mel Gibson blue. In fact, this Marine favored Mel in several ways—same color brown hair, same square jaw, same humorous glint in his so-blue eyes. Although she could have sworn that she'd seen a glimpse of panic when he'd first entered the room, now she thought she must have imagined it.

He had the same erect military posture of most Marines, but Joe Wilder had something else. A presence. The kids noticed it. They'd quieted noticeably since his arrival.

The khaki service uniform he wore, with its crisp shirt and matching tie and web belt with darker trousers, wasn't the best color in the world on most men, but she doubted anything looked bad on this man.

And she was stuck spending the weekend with him. Some women might dream of spending time with a sexy man in uniform. Not her.

"Sorry for the confusion, ma'am," Joe was saying, his voice as smooth as the rest of him. "When your father referred to you as his little princess, I naturally thought…"

"The wrong thing," she interrupted him to say. She hated her father's nickname for her. Little Princess. Just hearing it set her teeth on edge.

"I see that now." The earlier once-over visual he'd given her was back, only much more restrained now that he knew she was his commanding officer's daughter. Prudence was used to that information making a difference with men—with Marines in particular. Which was one of the major reasons she avoided contact with them.

She'd agreed to have Sergeant Brown accompany her on this field trip because she'd known the man since she was a kid. He was as old as her father and a personal friend.

The same was not true of Joe Wilder.

She'd have to tell her father he wouldn't do for this assignment. He'd have to find her someone else. Until then, they might as well begin the tour of the base. There was no reason Joe couldn't do that. She'd then speak to her father about a replacement for the remainder of the weekend.

"Okay, class, listen up now. Sergeant Wilder is here to begin our tour of the base. He's going to give you some background information about the history of the base and then begin the actual tour. Go ahead, Sergeant Wilder."

She was a bit surprised by the deer-in-the-headlights look Joe gave the gathered group of twenty-five kids. Maybe speaking in front of a group wasn't his thing? But then a Marine never showed any fear. And Joe was no different. His voice was strong, his demeanor confident as he began speaking.

"Listen up, everyone. You may address me as either Sergeant Wilder or sir. I'd like to welcome you all today to Camp Lejeune, a United States Marine Corps base, where we train the Marine Air/Ground Task Forces defending our country. Okay, let's start the tour." He seemed in a big hurry to get out of the small conference room all of a sudden.

"First tell the class a bit more about the base's history," Prudence suggested.

"Well," he drawled, "the base has been here a long time, ma'am."

"How long?" she pressed, enjoying putting him on the spot. There was something about the confidently sexy smile he'd flashed at her when he'd first walked into the room that had irked her. Equally irritating was her own response, the quickening of her heartbeat, the awareness of his vivid blue eyes and good looks.

And then there was that moment when he'd leaned close as if to kiss her. She hadn't been expecting that. She'd gotten used to men keeping their distance.

Turning to the class, Joe said, "Anyone know how long the base has been here?"

Two hands shot up. Since Joe had asked the question, she let him select which student would answer. He picked Pete Greene, a whiz with facts and figures. "Since World War Two, uh, 1941 to be exact, sir."

"Okay, let's start the tour," Joe said again.

Prudence held out a hand, stopping the mass exodus. "I think the class would like to know where the base got its name."

"Why did they name it after a legume?" Rosa Santos asked. "Aren't peanuts legumes?"

"It's Lejeune, dummy," Pete replied on Joe's behalf. "And it's huge, over 153,000 acres."

Sinatra Washington raised his hand, his silver-rimmed glasses glinting against his dark mocha complexion. "Sergeant Wilder, tell them about the fifty-four live-fire ranges, eighty-nine maneuver areas, thirty-three gun positions and twenty-five tactical landing zones."

"Maybe you should lead this tour," Joe replied. "Where did you get all that information?"

"From the Internet, sir." Sinatra, one of her most curious students and an avid fan of the Internet, held up the sheet of paper he'd printed from his computer.

Not wanting to be left behind in any statistical discussion, Pete said, "I read about that, too. You both failed to mention the state-of-the-art Military Operations in Urban Terrain training facility."

"I'm telling you, these kids don't need me here at all." Joe's voice may have been filled with humorous teasing, but she suspected there was an underlying element of fact there. He didn't want to be here. He wasn't comfortable around the kids. Oh, he tried not to show it, but there was a definite tenseness in his stance.

"Camp Lejeune has a self-guided tour with twenty-five points of interest," Sinatra stated.

"Self-guided, huh?" Joe repeated.

"Yes, sir. There's even a tour book that coordinates with the signs for each numbered point of interest."

"Self-guided. Well, that's great. Then you definitely don't need me," Joe stated with a hearty laugh.

"You're here to answer any questions," Prudence reminded him.

He wanted to tell her that to do that he'd have to

have access to the tour book, which the kid with the glasses and strange name seemed to have printed off the Internet. He wanted to tell her that he'd only been at the base a few weeks, he wanted to tell her he wasn't as dumb as he sounded. But most of all he wanted to get the heck out of here. Which meant starting the tour, whether he knew what he was talking about or not.

"This building houses base headquarters," Joe said as he opened the door and headed down the hallway. If the kids wanted to follow him, fine. No way was he staying in that tiny claustrophobic room with twenty-five kids a second longer. Flirting with her had distracted him for a while, but now that he knew the sexy teacher was off-limits, he didn't have anything to keep his mind off of the panic.

"The outside of the building looks like my church, only bigger," Rosa said as she followed him into the hallway, as did all the other kids and along with their rebellious teacher. "Redbrick with that fancy white thing on top."

"A cupola." At least that was one answer he could supply.

Rosa frowned up at Joe. "I thought he was the director of the movie *The Godfather*."

"That's Francis Ford Coppola," Pete said, rolling his eyes at her.

"An easy mistake to make," Joe said, wanting to keep moving. "As I said, you're inside Base Headquarters. From here the Commanding General oversees the daily workings of the entire base."

"And how many Marines would that include?" Prudence asked.

The teacher had it out for him. Joe could tell by the

questions she asked and by the way her lush mouth turned up in what he was coming to believe was a diabolical, if sexy, smile each time she asked them.

Fine, honey. Two can play at that game.

"Sinatra, how many Marines would that be?" Joe said.

Consulting his printout first, Sinatra said, "Approximately fifty thousand Marines, Navy personnel, civilian employees and military families, sir."

Joe liked this kid. As they passed the front lobby with its small display of historical swords, Sinatra discreetly passed him a copy of the self-guided tour book.

"Thanks," Joe murmured.

"I know what's it's like to be picked on," Sinatra told him with a reassuring smile.

Jeez, he'd come to this. A middle school teacher was picking on him. Him. Joe Wilder. An experienced United States Marine. Being picked on, not picked *up* as was often the case, by a woman. A sexy woman. A woman who was completely off-limits to him, seeing as how she was his commanding officer's "little princess."

He had to find a way to get out of this assignment.

The tour went more smoothly once he had the guidebook in his possession. He was able to tell the class about the massive live oak tree that was estimated to be over 350 years old. When one cocky kid asked him for the Latin name of the tree, he was even able to give that—*Quercus virginiana.*

Things got a little trickier in the barracks. There was something unexpectedly provocative about being with Prudence in a room filled with so many mattresses. Maybe he wasn't as bad off as he thought if he could think of sex at a time like this.

Of course, another way of looking at things was that he was truly certifiable to be entertaining the thought of his commanding officer's daughter and the word *sex* in the same sentence.

And then there were all the kids, swarming around in masses and sucking all the oxygen from the room.

"These beds are so little," Pete noted in surprise. "And they're bunk beds."

"Here in the Marine Corps, your bed is your rack," Joe automatically corrected him.

"A rack, huh? It looks like something you'd get tortured on," Pete agreed.

Torture was being in such close confines with so many kids. Even his first day of boot camp hadn't made him this jumpy.

"These beds...er, racks," Pete quickly corrected himself, "are really clean."

"That's because Marines have to learn how to make perfectly folded forty-five-degree corners on the sheets when they make their racks," Prudence said.

"No way!" Pete's brown eyebrows shot up. "Marines have to make beds...er...racks?"

"Affirmative," Joe said. "They have to learn the Marine way of making their racks."

"You see, in the Marine Corps there's only one right way of doing things and that's the Marine way," Prudence said in a mocking voice. Turning to Joe she said, "Tell the kids about the rest of Marine terminology. The floor is called..."

She was the daughter of a Marine, she knew what it was called. She simply wanted to wipe the deck with him. Daddy's little princess, indeed. Spoiled rotten needed to be added to that description. How dare she mock his beloved Marine Corps? He and the men she mocked put their lives on the line to protect her little fanny. But did she care? Clearly not.

Narrowing his eyes at her, Joe straightened his already ramrod straight shoulders. "The floor is a deck," he barked, startling her. Good. "To your right and left are bulkheads, not walls. Windows are ports. Above is an overhead, not a ceiling. Upstairs and downstairs do not exist. Instead we use topside and down below. You are facing forward. To your left is port and to your right is starboard. Behind you is aft."

"My dad has a boat and he uses those words," Pete said, hurriedly adding, "sir."

"The terms are a result of the Marine Corps early origins as a sea service," Joe said.

The tour ended at the Beirut Memorial, commemorating those who died in the 1983 bombing of Battalion Landing Team 1/8's Headquarters in Lebanon. Joe found it impossible to speak. For once, Prudence was quiet.

By the time the class returned to base headquarters, Joe had regained his self-control. He fielded the kids' questions as best he could on everything from the possibility of a top secret Marine Corps group that trained to protect earth from extraterrestrial life-forms to why his uniform was green.

During that time, Prudence kept her distance. He could tell she didn't like him. Which was fine by him. Maybe it would get him off this assignment.

Baby-sitting a bunch of sixth-graders was hardly up his alley. He'd been trained in hand-to-hand combat, in Marine battle tactics and camouflage and survival techniques. Not kid stuff.

Especially not now.

A few years ago Joe might have laughed off this

chore. But since the accident, his life had turned up-side down. And he was the only one who knew it. Which is the way he planned on keeping things.

"Daddy, this isn't going to work," Prudence stated as she perched herself on the corner of his desk.

"Hey, princess, how did the tour go?"

"The man you sent didn't know much about the base."

"Well, he's only been here a few weeks. Give the guy a chance."

She shook her head, sliding a strand of her dark hair behind one ear before saying, "I think it would be better if you found someone else for the job."

"Did Sergeant Wilder tell you to come talk to me on his behalf?" her father asked suspiciously.

"No." The question surprised her. "What makes you say that?"

"The fact that he's no more pleased about being given this assignment than you are about having him along."

"There you go then," Prudence said. "All the more reason to get someone else. You've got thousands of Marines here."

"I'm not the base commander here, princess. I was lucky to get Sergeant Wilder for this assignment on such short notice. I'm afraid you'll have to cancel the field trip if you don't take him." Pausing, he looked over her shoulder to the open doorway. "Ah, here he is now. Come on in, Sergeant."

"I'm sorry to interrupt, sir," Joe said, noting the cozy father-daughter setup.

"You're not interrupting. My daughter was just

talking about you. She's not happy at having you assigned to accompany her.''

"I'm sorry to hear that, sir." What a lie! The truth was that Joe was filled with relief. "I'm sure you'll find someone else...."

"Nonsense," his commanding officer said. "As I was just telling my daughter, it's you or no one."

Joe's heart fell.

Prudence looked equally disappointed with the news. "We're not canceling this trip," she said. "These kids have been looking forward to this for weeks."

"Twenty-five kids in the Blue Ridge mountains is a bit much for two adults to supervise, don't you think?" Joe said, still holding out a slim chance of escaping.

"Absolutely," Prudence agreed, the first time she'd agreed with anything he'd said all day. "Which is why there will only be five students coming on the field trip. The entire class got to come on the tour of the base, but participation in the field trip to the mountains was limited to the top five finalists in our Class Knowledge Fair." Hopping off her father's desk, she kissed her dad on the cheek before turning to face Joe. "I guess it looks like we're stuck with each other."

Chapter Three

"I can't believe you're actually calling *me* for help," Curt Blackwell noted, his amusement apparent over the phone line.

A year ago Joe had stood up at Curt's wedding as his best man. Funny how things changed. In the past, Curt had always been the loner and Joe the life of the party. Now Curt was happily married and had a young daughter named Blue. And it was Joe who was struggling.

"This has got to be a first," Curt was saying. "Usually it's the other way around, me calling you."

"Yeah, well, enjoy it while you can, buddy, because it's not going to happen very often. Not if you gloat like this every time I call you looking for some help."

"I won't gloat every time," Curt replied. "Just *this* time."

"There's no time for gloating. Just think of some way I can get out of this stupid mess."

"A Marine never avoids an assignment."

"He does if it involves escorting his commanding officer's daughter into the mountains of North Carolina for the weekend."

"How old is she?" Curt asked.

"I don't know. Late twenties, I'd guess."

"Sounds like a plum assignment for a ladies' man like you. What's the problem?"

"She's bringing some of her sixth-grade class with her. She's a teacher. And we didn't exactly hit it off."

"What?" Curt sounded mockingly incredulous. "Another first! A woman who doesn't fall at your feet? Wait till I tell Jessie."

"This is privileged material," Joe said emphatically. "So don't go blabbing anything to that cute wife of yours."

"Since when are the details of your sex life a matter of national security?" Curt retorted.

"Since they involved the daughter of my C.O." Joe used the abbreviation for commanding officer.

"I guess you do have a point there. Okay, this will remain between the two of us."

"Fine. Now give me an idea of how to get out of this."

"If the order is an illegal one..."

"Don't I wish," Joe muttered. "But last time I checked there was no law against getting stuck with a spoiled, sexy teacher who has it in for me. Nor is it illegal to be called on to fill-in for a public affairs officer who needed emergency surgery and couldn't lead this weekend excursion himself. The order isn't illegal, just a pain in the butt."

"Did you mention that you haven't been posted down there in North Carolina very long—"

"Affirmative," Joe interrupted him to confirm. "Tried that approach. Unsuccessful."

"You said the daughter wasn't fond of you. Did you—?"

"Point that out? Affirmative," Joe again interrupted. "Deemed irrelevant by the C.O."

"Then I guess you're stuck."

"Gee, thanks, that was real helpful, Blackwell," Joe said sarcastically. "I'm so glad I called you."

Curt laughed. "Hey, anytime I can help, I'm just a phone call away."

Joe's growl didn't need translating.

"You're stuck, Wilder," Curt said. "Make the most of it is my advice to you. *Semper Gumby,* buddy. Be flexible."

"Yeah, right." Frustrated, Joe flipped the cover on his cellular phone and stared at the bag he had packed while talking to Curt. A Marine was always ready to leave, never knowing when some situation might require him to defend his country.

What about defending his sanity? Joe wondered caustically, furious with himself for feeling the way he did. What was the procedure for that?

He was a Marine, by God. There were no foxholes in the Marines. Foxholes are for those who want to hide. In the Marines they had *fighting* holes. There was no hiding in the Marines. He'd been trained to *fight.*

His father and his grandfather had been Marines. He was part of a proud tradition—the few, the proud, the Marines.

Joe glanced down at his watch. His allotted hour was almost up. Falling back on years of conditioning and training, he willed his misgivings away and completed packing with ruthless efficiency. The sooner he got started on this idiotic assignment, the sooner it would be over with.

Joe Wilder was late. Prudence couldn't believe it. Marines were rarely late. Commissioned officers or enlisted men—it didn't matter. They tended to work with military precision. Especially those in her father's command.

Maybe Joe had chickened out? Yeah, right.

Or maybe he'd come up with someone else to take his place? Yeah, right. As if he'd disobey an order.

Or maybe that was him over there talking to Sinatra...

Yes, it most certainly was.

So why hadn't Joe alerted her to his presence instead of letting her stand around like a doofus waiting for him? There was just something about him that set her teeth on edge.

From the moment he'd walked into that conference room and flashed his confident smile at her, she'd known that this was a man used to getting his own way where women were concerned. She'd seen the type before.

Yes, he was better looking than most men. And, yes, he had incredible blue eyes. But there was no way she was going to be swayed by a man in uniform. She'd been down that path before.

Joe Wilder might not have been at the base very long, but already he had the reputation for being a heartbreaking daredevil. At one point his wild ways would have appealed to her, but she'd grown up since then and those days were long gone.

Being stuck out in the wilds on the North Carolina mountains with a sexy Marine was one of her worst nightmares. That and spiders. She'd always been a sissy about spiders. Snakes and other bugs didn't bother her one little bit. But spiders gave her the willies.

Even a sexy Marine was better than getting stuck with spiders. Besides, the bottom line here was that she was immune to the charms of any man in a uniform. She'd been played for a fool once by Steven Banks, who had professed to love her but had really been looking to pay back her father. Steven, a commissioned Navy officer who'd gone to Annapolis, hadn't appreciated the lukewarm performance evaluation her father, an enlisted man and a Marine to boot, had given him. So he'd gotten even by going after Prudence behind her father's back.

Prudence didn't intend to make the same mistake twice by getting involved with another military man. She was currently dating a very nice teacher named George Rimes. He was quiet and studious. A birdwatcher. He'd wanted to accompany her this weekend but had had to return home to Iowa for a family wedding.

And so she was stuck with Joe Wilder—who was as far off the high end of the masculinity spectrum as you could get from shy George.

"Sergeant Wilder, are you ready to go?" Her voice reflected her impatience.

"Yes, ma'am."

His words didn't sound too convincing to her, although they were delivered in a Marine's clipped voice. "Good."

She'd already run through the detailed checklist she had on her clipboard twice, covering everything from sleeping bags to sunblock, to make sure that none of her students had forgotten anything.

She also had signed parental approval forms from everyone. She'd wanted to include a parent for the outing, but none had volunteered or even been willing to be drafted. Which left her and Joe Wilder as the only adults accompanying the five students. Of course, Joe was a Marine so that meant he probably counted as two adults...as least as far as *he* was concerned. Marines were nothing if not confident. "Then let's get in the van, everyone."

Joe quickly stowed his gear in the back of the van, which was already packed tight, and then headed for the driver's seat.

"I'm driving," Prudence informed him.

"She's a good driver," Sinatra told Joe reassuringly. "For a teacher."

"Thanks for the vote of confidence, Sinatra," Prudence said. "Sergeant, you no doubt remember Sinatra, Rosa and Pete from the tour we took a short while ago."

Joe nodded. Sinatra was the one who'd taken pity on him, Pete was the whiz with facts and figures and Rosa was the one with the unusual questions. He didn't recognize the other two kids, though. One was an Asian kid with a short buzz haircut and a silver earring in his left ear. The other was an African-American girl who was eyeing him with blatant skepticism while proudly wearing an I'm Mean And Green T-shirt. But then he hadn't really been paying attention to the entire herd of kids. After the first minute or two their faces had blurred as he'd focused on maintaining his control.

"This is Keishon Williams," Prudence said, putting

her hand on the girl's shoulder. "And this is Gem Wong," she added, turning to the boy with the earring.

"Nice tattoo, sir," Gem noted with a nod at the eagle on Joe's upper arm.

"Nice earring," Joe said in return.

The kid grinned, the flash of sunlight off his silver braces nearly blinding Joe. Time for more aspirin. His post-hangover headache was coming back. And the thought of being in the passenger seat while the sexy but infuriating teacher drove the van didn't help improve his mood any.

"I can drive," Joe said, hoping against hope that she'd give in.

"I'm sure you can," she replied. "I heard about your motorcycle racing escapades."

"You race motorcycles? Awesome," Pete asked.

"You don't trust me, ma'am?" Joe asked her.

She sidestepped answering that one. "It's my van. I'll drive. That way, while we're en route, Sergeant Wilder can give you some wilderness tips for our weekend."

"When they trained you in survival stuff in the Marines, did you have to eat live bugs like those guys on that TV show where they were stuck on an island?" Pete asked.

"Larva," Sinatra corrected him.

"I read on the Internet that you shouldn't eat mice because you could get some disease," Pete said.

"I wouldn't eat mice because I'm a vegetarian," Keishon stated with a shudder.

Pete grinned. "You'd eat 'em if you were hungry enough."

Infuriated by his attitude, Keishon yelled, "Would not!"

"Would so!" Pete shouted right back.

"Williams and Greene, cease and desist!" Joe barked.

The two kids looked at him in astonishment before Keishon loftily informed him, "It's not nice to call someone by their last name."

It wasn't nice for them to argue when his head felt like it was going to detonate. But then the world wasn't a nice place. The sooner they knew that the better.

How was he going to manage cooped up in this tin can of a van with five kids for hours?

He just had to stop thinking of them as kids and instead treat them as recruits. Really short recruits. Maybe that would help his stress level.

He'd dealt with raw recruits before.

"Isn't this van equipped with a video player?" Pete asked.

"She won't let us watch *The Matrix*," Gem quietly complained.

"I've already seen it ten times," Pete bragged.

"Then you don't need to see it again," Prudence said. "Instead I want you to notice how the trees change as we head away from the coast and head for the mountains."

"That was some big bad kind of tree on the base," Sinatra noted.

"It's 350 years old," Pete said.

"That was just an estimate," Rosa reminded them.

"Now she'll probably tell us how many inches the tree grows every year," Pete said in exasperation. "She's the class math whiz."

"So why were you all chosen for this mission?" Joe had almost slipped up and called them kids. Mistake. Short recruits. Really short recruits, that's what they were.

Not that the image was helping as much as it should.

"We are the five finalists in our class Knowledge Fair. Our projects were chosen by Principal Vann as the best," Sinatra proudly stated. "We had to come up with a hypothesis and then try and prove it was true. Mine was that the Internet improves kids' grades if they use it for researching science homework projects."

"My hypothesis is that a vegetarian diet is healthier than a nonvegetarian one," Keishon said.

"Mine was that the hole in the ozone layer is changing the climate," Pete said. "Gem's was about the life cycle of a frog and Rosa's was about using rings in a tree to figure its age."

"Do you do have to do a hypothesis to be in the Marines?" Rosa asked him. "Do you have to prove that something is true?"

Did he have something to prove? Constantly. Corps values—honor, courage, commitment—were the lifeblood of a Marine. From the second a recruit stepped off the bus at Marine Corp Recruit Depot the Marine Corps created a change of mind, body and spirit meant to last a lifetime. They were constantly taking on challenges that proved a recruit was worthy of being called a United States Marine.

Did he have something to prove? You bet. Was he still worthy? Joe didn't know...and that was one of the many things eating away at him.

"In the Marines, do you have tests like we have in school?" Rosa continued.

Focus on the facts and figures, he ordered himself.

"Boot camp has five graduation requirements—rifle qualification, swim qualification, a physical fitness test, battalion-commander's inspection and scoring eighty percent on academic tests."

"Eighty percent isn't that good," Keishon pointed out. "That would only be a *B* in our class."

"Depending on the scores of the rest of the class," Rosa said. "Girls can be Marines, right?"

"Affirmative," Joe replied. "I pointed out their training area and barracks area during the base tour."

"Girls can be whatever they want to be," Prudence added.

"Were you ever a Marine?" Rosa asked her.

"No," Prudence replied. "I always wanted to be a teacher."

"There aren't any teachers in the Marines?" Rosa said.

Prudence shook her head. "Only drill instructors, and they aren't the same thing."

"I don't know," Joe drawled, giving her a wry look. "I can easily imagine you barking out orders in BWT, ma'am."

"What's BWT?" Pete asked, always eager to learn something new.

"Basic Warrior Training," Joe replied.

"You think Ms. Martin is a warrior?" Pete said.

Joe nodded. "She was raised by a warrior."

"That would be my mom," Prudence told her students. "Not that my dad is any slouch, either," she noted with a grin. "After all, he *is* a Marine."

"I was referring to your father," Joe said.

She gave him a mocking look. "No kidding."

"Is kidding allowed in the Marines?" Pete asked.

Joe thought back to the numerous practical jokes

he'd played on his brothers or his buddies over the years. "In very special circumstances and under certain conditions, then the answer is that sometimes kidding is allowed, yes."

Pete frowned. "I didn't think warriors were supposed to be kidding around."

"Sometimes laughter is the only thing that keeps you going when it seems impossible to continue," Joe quietly said, his smile disappearing. And sometimes even that didn't work.

The Fates had to be laughing their heads off at him, crammed in a tin can van with five kids and his C.O.'s daughter. Yeah, someone up there was no doubt having hysterics right about now.

Too bad Joe wasn't laughing with them. A year ago, none of this would have bothered him. But then Joe was a very different Marine than he'd been a year ago.

So far he seemed to be the only one aware of it. But that awareness was slowly eating away at him, along with the guilt and the secret shame that he was no longer good enough, strong enough, courageous enough to be called a United States Marine.

He bolted down those dark emotions and focused his attention on the passing scenery. They'd left the coastal plain and the short palmetto palms behind. They'd also passed the urban areas of Raleigh-Durham and Winston-Salem, traveling clear across the state until they were now surrounded by pine forests. The green foothills had given way to bigger mountains, their rounded curves flowing from one ridge to the next in layers of smoky-blue.

The kids...er...the very short recruits continued peppering him with questions for the remainder of the drive. Every so often, Joe would turn to look at Prudence to see if he could read her thoughts. She didn't talk much, letting him do the bulk of the work in responding to the questions being tossed his way by her *uber*curious students. The small smile on her lips made him think that she was enjoying putting him in the hot seat.

Looking at her mouth made him hot, hot in a different way. Hot to kiss her, hot to taste her mouth, part her lips with his tongue and...

Joe blinked. What was he doing? He had no business fantasizing about his commanding officer's daughter. No business at all.

Ordering his gaze away from her, he reminded himself that she was off-limits to him in every way.

"Is it true Marines have nicknames like Jughead?" Keishon said.

Joe tried not to wince. "Jarhead, not Jughead."

"What other nicknames do Marines have?"

"Devil Dogs," Joe replied.

"Sounds like a kind of hot dog they have at Dog 'n' Suds. I think it has hot peppers in it," Pete said.

Joe tried not to grit his teeth. "Sinatra, do you know why Marines are called Devil Dogs?"

"It better not be because they're mean to dogs," Keishon, the animal activist, said.

"Marines aren't mean to dogs. The name came from the Germans during the first World War," Sinatra proudly replied.

"*Teufelhunden,*" Joe said. "So named because of the Marines' tenacity in combat during the Battle of Belleau Wood. Nice going, Sinatra."

"Teacher's pet," Pete muttered.

"What was that?" Joe demanded, using his drill instructor voice.

"Nothing," Pete quickly replied. "I was just...
uh...coughing, sir."

Just when Joe was sure he couldn't stand being
cooped up with this bunch a second later, Prudence
cheerfully announced, "We're here!"

The Sunshine Trailhead wasn't nearly as impressive
as it sounded. In reality it was merely a graveled parking lot. But it represented the end of the line as far as
being stuck in this van with Pete, Keishon, Gem, Rosa
and Sinatra—not to mention their impossibly sexy
teacher Prudence.

Joe was the first one out of the van. As he watched
the really short recruits climbing out of the van, he
was reminded of circus routine he'd seen as a kid with
clowns tumbling out of a VW Bug.

This wasn't the most graceful bunch of really short
recruits he'd ever seen. Not that being graceful was
something a Marine aimed for, but this group seemed
to fall over their own feet an awful lot.

Meanwhile Prudence stood watch with a clipboard,
ticking off items as they were unpacked from the van.

"Six sleeping bags..." She paused to count them
off as each student donned their backpack. "Check.
Two tents. Check. Six backpacks. Check. I'm assum-
ing you're responsible for your own items, Sergeant
Wilder?"

"Affirmative," he replied, while efficiently adding
the larger of the tents to his pack.

Prudence watched him work, the muscles in his
arms rippling as he easily hefted the pack and put it
on. He didn't have the bulky frame of a football player
or wrestler, but he was powerfully built in a lean-and-
mean kind of way.

The sun had seared crinkles around his eyes, or

maybe those were laugh lines? She was only now no-
ticing that his nose and jaw weren't perfectly sym-
metrical, saving him from a merely pretty-boy hand-
someness. His was the face of a man who'd seen and
done more than his fair share of living.

He'd been fairly good-natured about the kids'
incessant questions during the drive. She was surprised. She shouldn't have been. Marines were infa-
mous for following orders and as Joe had told her
more than once, he'd been ordered to accompany her
and her students on this field trip.

But that didn't mean he'd grown any more comfortable with the situation. She still didn't know what
it was about the kids that made him uneasy. Maybe
he was an only child or something and didn't have
much experience with kids.

She could ask him, she supposed. But she was hesitant to form a friendship with him. She didn't want
to know if he was an only child, didn't want to know
why his nose was a little off-kilter. The man himself
made her feel off-kilter all the time. Keeping her distance, emotionally even if she couldn't do that physically, was clearly the wise thing to do in this situation.

Yes, she was spending the weekend in the mountains with him, but they were being chaperoned by five
sixth-graders. And it wasn't as if she was dressed like
a fashion model or anything. Her hardy hiking boots
were hardly the thing to turn a man's head. She was
wearing the same khaki slacks and white T-shirt she'd
had on earlier. She'd added a long-sleeved denim shirt
and tied a red windbreaker around her waist.

Glancing at her reflection in the van's outside mirror, she adjusted the silver hair clip she'd fastened her
hair back with before turning to inspect her students.

She checked each child's backpack to make sure it was properly positioned, wasn't too heavy and that the straps weren't twisted.

Finally they headed off, with Joe in the front and Prudence bringing up the rear. From this vantage point she watched Joe. She'd always had a thing for guys in jeans, which is why she was surprised to find her heartbeat quickening. The man was wearing camouflage utilities, for heaven's sake. Camies. Hardly sexy attire. But it was the man not the uniform that was getting to her. It was the man who was getting *away* from her as he set a pace much too fast for this group.

"Sergeant, we're not on an enforced march here," she called out. "We're supposed to be enjoying the wilderness, not marching through it double-time."

Joe shortened his usual long stride and fast tempo in order for the others to keep up with him. Even so, Prudence wasn't satisfied, as she indicated when they took their first rest stop.

"Sergeant, you're supposed to be leading the troop," she said, "not running away from us."

Her words were a deliberate red flag. A Marine never ran away from anything.

Prudence was trying to taunt him. He refused to give her the satisfaction of reacting.

Ignoring her comment, he spoke to the really short recruits, addressing them as if they were "poolies"— high school seniors who'd signed up for delayed entry into the Marine Corps upon graduation. "While we're paused here, I'll review the Marine Corps Survival techniques. Think of the word Survival. *S* stands for *Sizing Up The Situation.*"

The situation was that Joe was stuck in the mountains with a forbidden woman and five kids.

Shoving that thought aside, Joe asked. "What can you hear and see?"

"I hear birds and the wind in the trees," Sinatra said.

"And I see a squirrel on that tree over there," Rosa said.

"What about smell?" Joe asked.

"Hey, I took a shower this morning," Pete declared. "I don't smell."

Joe stifled a laugh. "Close your eyes and sniff the air. What can you smell?"

"Pine. I smell pine," Pete replied. "What about you, sir? What do you smell?"

Perfume. Joe smelled Prudence's perfume. Like Al Pacino in that movie, Joe was pretty good at identifying a woman's perfume. But this one had him stymied. It was something citrusy with a bit...of cinnamon maybe?

Erase that thought, Joe ordered himself. He refused to allow her entry into his thoughts. And if she barged into his thoughts, he vowed to toss her out.

"I smell pine, too," Joe replied. "Now *U* stands for *Undue Haste Makes Waste.*"

"My point exactly," Prudence inserted.

"*R* stands for *Remember Where You Are.*" Joe pointed to the topographical hiking map he had with him. "Orient yourself to the terrain, like that mountain over there."

"The mountains all look the same," Pete said.

"Not if you look closely," Joe said. "See how it has that stand of bare trees near the top?"

"Probably killed by acid rain," Keishon stated darkly.

Joe continued, "*V* stands for *Vanquishing Fear and*

Panic.'' Yeah, right. This was one Joe had to work on himself, big-time. He shoved those thoughts aside. ''*I* stands for *Improvise. V* stands for *Value Living* and *A* for *Act Like Natives.*''

''What's that supposed to mean?'' Keishon said. ''What natives live in the mountains?''

''Animals,'' Gem replied on Joe's behalf. ''Animals live in the mountains.''

''And animals are smarter than people,'' Keishon said. ''They know stuff, like where water is, right?''

''That's right,'' Joe said. ''So we've covered *S…U…R…V…I…V…A.* Which leaves us with?''

''*L*,'' Sinatra supplied.

''And *L* stands for *Live by Your Wits,*'' Joe concluded. ''Learning basic skills helps you develop your self-confidence.''

Sinatra nodded. ''I checked out some camping Web sites and learned about wilderness skills stuff. It made me feel better about this trip, made me look forward to it more.''

Keishon added, ''And Ms. Martin covered other information in class.''

Covered…oh, yes, he'd like to see Ms. Martin covered, all right. Covered in yards and yards of concealing material, because maybe then he wouldn't notice the way her T-shirt molded the curve of her breasts. He was watching the woman breathe, for God's sake. Not a good sign.

''All right, recruits,'' Joe barked. ''Time to move out!'' And time for him to remember the goals of his mission this weekend where Prudence Martin was concerned—survival, not seduction.

Chapter Four

"I don't agree," Prudence was saying.

Surprise, surprise, Joe irritably thought to himself. His C.O.'s little princess hadn't agreed with one single thing he'd done or said for the past two hours.

Pointing to a spot just to her right in the opposite direction of the place Joe had chosen, she said, "I think this campsite is better."

"It is if you want the cold night air blowing through your tent. The prevailing winds here are from the west, which means you don't want the entrance to your tent facing that way. Ma'am," he added.

"Why didn't you just say why you wanted the tent placed the way you did in the first place?" she asked in exasperation before holding up her hand like a cop stopping traffic. "Never mind, I know the answer to that question. Because you're a Marine and you're used to having your orders blindly obeyed." Placing her hands on her slender hips, she said, "Well, I'm not one of your recruits."

"No kidding, ma'am," he drawled respectfully, unable to stop himself from appreciating what a pretty picture she made, standing there all flushed and riled up.

"So let's both keep in mind the reason we're here."

"Because your father, my commanding officer, ordered me to be here, ma'am," he said.

"To give the kids an educational and enjoyable outing," she corrected him. "They worked hard on their science projects and I don't want anything ruining this weekend for them." Her gaze was direct, her chocolate-brown eyes unwavering. "So what do you say we call a temporary truce?" She held out her hand. "For the kids. Shall we shake on it?"

There was no reason for Joe to hesitate. No reason to expect the powerful jolt of sexual attraction that slammed into him at the feel of her slender fingers curled around his hand. But it was there. Unmistakable. Ferocious. Unsettling.

Studying her face, he saw that Prudence felt it, too. There was a startled yet intrigued look in her eyes that he found incredibly appealing. He'd found plenty of women sexy in the past, but none of them had made him feel downright bedazzled the way she did.

Danger, Joe Wilder! The silent warning shot through his mind and he dropped her hand as if it were a live grenade.

Sure, Joe liked a challenge, especially one that involved a good-looking woman, but he was no dummy. This wasn't a challenge, it was professional suicide.

Taking any action on the sizzling chemistry crackling between them would be a speedy one-way ticket right out of the Marines. Her father would see to that. Not that there was any regulation against dating your

C.O.'s daughter; it was one of those unspoken rules like not putting your hand in a raging inferno. Common sense dictated you didn't do stupid things like that.

And Joe had plenty of common sense. Or at least he always had in the past.

Stepping away from her, he concentrated on getting the two tents up, making sure the very short recruits assisted.

Watching him supervise the kids, Prudence rubbed her fingers, which still hummed from his touch. He had a large hand, but it wasn't his handshake that had been overpowering. No, it was Joe that was overpowering. And not just in a physical way, although she was extremely aware of him physically.

The camies and field jacket he wore were hardly the most sexy attire. And it wasn't as if she hadn't seen thousands of Marines dressed identically in her lifetime. But there was something about *this* Marine that got to her.

Maybe it was his Mel Gibson blue eyes or the slight dimple at the right of his mouth when he smiled. There was just something about him...

It certainly wasn't his way with kids. He was still on edge around them.

Oh, it wasn't noticeable if you weren't looking. But she *was* looking, that was the problem. She was looking at Joe Wilder entirely too much.

Asking Gem and Keishon to help her, she gathered firewood for a campfire. The campsite already had an area for fires designated by a ring of large rocks. By the time they had a healthy-size fire going, the tents were up and the sleeping bags stowed.

As twilight fell, she tried not to notice the fact that

Joe looked good in the firelight. But he kept his distance, not quite joining in with the rest of them. The kids had enjoyed their dinner of hot dogs and potato chips. Their fruit drinks came in a container with a straw so there was no need for cups or glasses, which made cleaning up a breeze. Tomorrow night's meal— powdered beef stew—probably wouldn't be as big a hit with the kids as tonight's.

Joe had positioned the two tents so that the smoke from the fire didn't constantly blow into them. She wasn't sure why she'd argued with him about its location in the first place. He got to her and set her off like flint striking sparks.

She was just glad that he'd dropped his flirtatious act, the one he'd used on her when he'd first walked into that conference room back at the base. But that had been before he'd known that she was his commanding officer's daughter. Ever since then he'd been propriety itself. Which made the awareness between them all the more puzzling. He clearly didn't want to feel anything toward her and she felt the same about him. You'd think that would be enough to keep sexual chemistry at bay. And if that didn't, the fact that they were surrounded by her students would be sufficient to squelch any romantic notions.

"While there's still enough light from the fire, why don't you all take out your journals and write down your notes for today?" Prudence suggested. "Here, Sergeant, I brought a notebook so you could join in with this exercise and write down your thoughts."

"That wasn't necessary, ma'am."

Waving the notebook at him, she said, "I wouldn't want you to feel left out."

"I'm not the sensitive type, ma'am."

Seeing she wasn't about to back down, he took the notebook from her, taking care not to touch her fingertips. What was it about this woman that got to him so? She was cute, but not the most beautiful woman he'd ever met.

No, it was more than just her physical appearance. It was everything about her—her attitude, her way of handling the very short recruits, her insistence on needling him.

"Sir, do Marines know how to navigate from the stars?" Gem asked Joe, interrupting his train of thought.

But even as Joe pointed out the North Star and how to find it in the night sky, a part of his mind remained on Prudence. The group didn't seem to notice his distraction, but then he was good at hiding his emotions.

"You can see the Milky Way from here. With all those galaxies up there, there's no way we're the only ones in the universe," Gem said.

"What do you think aliens really look like?" Rosa asked.

"I liked the aliens in *Men in Black*." This from Pete.

Keishon wrinkled her nose and shook her head. "They were too slimy and gross."

"How do you know we don't look gross to them?" Pete countered.

"They haven't seen us," Keishon replied.

"Sure they have. Don't you read those newspapers at the supermarket? Don't you know about *Roswell?* Or *The X-Files?* The aliens are here among us all right," Pete said.

"Maybe you're one of them," Keishon retorted. "You sure act strange enough." Turning to Joe she said, "What do you think, Sergeant? Do you think there is intelligent life in outer space?"

She was asking this of a guy who wasn't always even sure there was intelligent life on earth. Joe looked up at the stars and was suddenly reminded of an incident when he was a little kid—when his dad had taken him outside and shown him the Big Dipper. He remembered the awe he'd felt. He hadn't thought of that for decades. And that awe and sense of wonder had long since disappeared. "I don't know," Joe said.

"The Marines don't deal with aliens, the Air Force does," Pete told Keishon. "You'd know that if you watched more TV."

Ignoring him, Keishon spoke to Joe. "Who's Alice? I heard you talking about her before."

"I wasn't talking about a female," Joe said.

"You know a guy named Alice?" Pete asked, one brown eyebrow raised so high it almost disappeared beneath his Carolina Panthers cap.

"ALICE is my pack," Joe said.

Pete's disbelief turned into doubt. "You name your backpack?"

"ALICE is an acronym for All-purpose Lightweight Individual Carrying Equipment," Joe explained.

Keishon frowned. "Don't you think it would have been easier to just call it a backpack?"

"Marines don't do things just because it might be easier that way," Prudence mockingly noted. "They also have a thing for acronyms."

"We talked about acronyms in class. I use them. They help me remember things," Gem said.

"My palm computer helps me remember things," Sinatra said, patting one of the many pockets on his khaki vest where he kept his prized possession.

"Computers are fine, but you have to be able to survive without them," Joe said. "You have to depend on your own skills." A Marine never depended on anything but his fellow Marines.

Joe tensed against the all-too-familiar pain as emotions hit him like a kick in the gut. He'd let his fellow Marines down. There should have been something he could have done instead of standing there helplessly, a witness to the horrendous accident as the helo went down in flames.

"The fire is dying down," Rosa noted.

"That's fine," Joe curtly replied. The fire reminded him too much of the fiery crash. Every damn thing reminded him. "It's just about time to hit the rack anyway."

"That means bed," Rosa said triumphantly, clearly pleased with herself at being able to translate "Marine-speak" into English.

"If the fire goes out, we won't be able to see in the dark." Keishon didn't sound too thrilled by that prospect.

"Sure you can," Joe replied, going on automatic pilot. "After one minute of darkness the eyes' sensitivity to light increases ten times. After twenty minutes, it increases six thousand times." Facts and figures were all he had to hold on to sometimes.

"And after forty minutes, it achieves the maximum sensitivity increasing…twenty-five thousand times!" Sinatra stated with a dramatic flair.

"Awesome," Gem said, his earring and silver braces gleaming in the dying firelight.

"How did you know that?" Pete demanded.

"I looked it up on my palm computer," Sinatra

admitted, holding it out for them to see. "I down-loaded info into it before I left."

To which Joe said, "I'll bet your palm computer doesn't tell you that it's possible, from a mountaintop on a night like tonight, to detect the flare of a match fifty miles away."

"No, it didn't tell me that, but I just entered that info," Sinatra said.

"So if we don't see anything, does that mean there's nobody around us for fifty miles?" Keishon asked.

"We'd have to stay out here for forty minutes in order for our eyes to be completely adjusted to the darkness," Prudence said.

"Well, I'm not sitting out here in the dark for that long," Keishon declared, jumping to her feet.

"She's afraid of bears," Pete said.

"I am not," Keishon angrily denied.

"Are, too."

"If you keep dissing me, the Sergeant is gonna yell at you again," Keishon warned Pete with a meaningful look in Joe's direction.

"He yelled at *both* of us before," Pete reminded her.

"He did not," Keishon said.

"He did so."

When Joe glared at both of them over the rim of the metal cup holding his instant coffee, their arguing instantly stopped. He'd learned that look from a drill instructor at boot camp who'd had a way of looking at recruits as if they'd been sent from Hades to torment drill instructors. Joe could relate. These kids were driving him up a wall.

So was the idea of being stuck in the tent with the

three boys. It wasn't that he valued his privacy. A Marine checked his privacy at the gate when he enlisted. It was the vertically challenged recruits. Or in acronym-loving Marine terms—VCR. That's what they were, a bunch of VCRs.

Joe would have preferred lying out under the stars, but Prudence was adamant about there being an adult in the male VCRs' tent. Prudence and the two female VCRs were in the smaller tent.

Joe was the last to turn in. Even so, he doubted he'd fall asleep.

He didn't even realize he'd dozed off...until the nightmare came.

It always started the same way. He saw the rotor blades gleaming in the sunlight as the helicopter took off. Then time and motion slowed as the Cobra lost power and fell to the earth. Flames shooting into the sky. Death. Destruction. Despair.

He woke gasping for air, beads of sweat clinging to his clammy forehead.

No matter how many times Joe relived the past, there was no way to undo it. And that was the torturous part of survival guilt. There was no way of fixing it. No way of making it better. No way of changing his bone-deep belief that if he'd been aboard maybe there would have been something he could have done to prevent the crash—that he could have saved those three Marines who'd died.

Desperately needing fresh air, Joe got up and slipped out of the tent. Clouds scuttled across the moon as he stared at the sky, gulping cold air as if he'd been suffocating.

"Testing your night vision, Sergeant?" Prudence inquired from behind him.

Immediately on alert, Joe pivoted like the warrior he was, ready to do battle.

"Whoa there," she said with a startled smile. "It's just me. Not the enemy. What's the matter? Couldn't sleep?"

"What are you doing out here?" he growled.

"I was enjoying the peace and quiet while I could. There isn't much of that with five sixth-graders around."

"You should hit the rack," he told her. "We've got an early start tomorrow."

"The kids seem to make you nervous," she noted, showing no signs of returning to her tent as he'd suggested. "Why is that?"

Joe wished he knew. But ever since the helo crash, kids freaked him out. Not only the sight of them, but also being responsible for them.

He'd first noticed the problem when he'd visited Curt and his new wife up in Chicago over a liberty weekend. Holding Curt's daughter, Blue, had made his knees tremble. Him, who'd always been good with females, from toddlers on up to grandmas. He'd always had a way with women and had never had any problems with kids. But that was the old Joe, the one that had gone up in flames along with that helo.

"Not everyone is good with kids, ma'am," Joe said stiffly.

"That's true," Prudence agreed. "But with you it seems like it's more than that." She paused, giving him the chance to speak up if he chose to. He didn't. "I meant to tell you that somehow your journal got picked up with Keishon's and Rosa's by mistake. It wasn't until I was reading it that I realized it was yours. I should have guessed from the writing. Why do all Marines have such small squiggly writing?'' she inquired in a teasing voice.

"Squiggly?" he repeated in disbelief, his shoulders straightening at what he perceived to be a new insult against his beloved Marine Corps. "There is no such word."

"There most certainly is," she assured him, dropping onto a large flat boulder in order to gaze up at him and at the sky.

"Fine, ma'am," he growled. "I'm not going to argue with you about it."

"Why not?" She turned to flash a grin at him in the moonlit darkness. "You argue about everything else with me."

"Only because you're wrong most of the time. Ma'am."

"You really don't have to continue saying ma'am to me," she told him. "I know it's only a facade of politeness that you don't mean a word of."

"So now you've added mind-reading to your other skills?" he said, moving closer to the boulder.

"What other skills might that be?"

"Besides the ability to aggravate me, you mean, ma'am?"

"Yes, besides that ability, Sergeant." She tilted her head up to look at him, now that he was so near. Her shoulder-length hair tumbled over her shoulders. She was wearing black sweatpants and a red sweatshirt with sheep on it.

"You seem to be a good teacher," he allowed grudgingly.

"You're too kind."

"So I've been told."

"And you're too good-looking," she stunned him

and herself by saying. "No doubt you've been told that as well."

"Not put that way, no."

"Put what way?"

"As if it were a sin."

He was sinfully good-looking, that much was true. The real reason she was out here was that she'd had the most disturbingly erotic dream about him. And that wasn't like her at all.

But then she hadn't been feeling quite like herself from the moment Joe Wilder had walked into that conference room back at the base. She couldn't believe she'd just told him he was too good-looking. She hadn't meant to. The words had just kind of slipped out.

There was something about talking to him in the darkness that made her forget her reservations. Which was a dangerous thing for her to do. She couldn't forget who he was. Not for one minute.

She might not be the enemy, but in a way he was. He was the enemy to her peace of mind, to the future she had planned for herself. A future without a too-sexy Marine with too-blue eyes playing any role in it.

"I think I will head back to my sleeping bag," she noted, hastily getting to her feet before realizing that he was now standing so close to the boulder that she almost slammed into him.

His hands automatically shot out to prevent her from stumbling over the uneven ground beneath their feet. "Steady there," he said.

It was an order she silently repeated to her own heartbeat, which was racing out of control. Powerful crosscurrents of emotion swept over her until her entire body was alive and flushed. She forgot to breathe, forgot to think as the immediate world skittered away. Her universe telescoped inward until it contained nothing beyond the intimate circle of his arms.

Then she was suddenly set free.

"You'd best get back to your tent, ma'am," he said in that ultrarespectful voice that Marines used.

Instead of arguing, she merely nodded. What had just happened? His touch had created a response she could neither understand nor control.

Hurrying back to her tent, Prudence paused in the entryway to look over her shoulder. Joe was walking away from her, a solitary figure melting into the darkness. Then he was gone.

But the vivid memory of his touch remained with her throughout the night.

The next day was blustery, cloudy and cool. Joe had checked the weather forecast before leaving the base and while there was a large storm out over the Atlantic, they were expecting it to continue north along the coast and not come inland.

Something about the sky made him uneasy. Maybe it was just the VCRs getting on his nerves, but he didn't think so.

He tried to keep the pace brisk, but Prudence insisted on stopping—to look at wildflowers, to take pictures of a waterfall, to explain an ecosystem. As it was, they barely managed to make camp that night before the rain hit. Joe dug a channel around the base of the tents, making sure it ran downhill to prevent flooding.

As he shoveled the dirt, Joe had a bad feeling about the weather. The air had turned decidedly colder. He only prayed that the rain wouldn't turn to snow.

His prayers were not answered. The rain turned to

snow a little after midnight. There was nothing he could do. He couldn't get the VCRs moving in the dark, even with flashlights. They were simply too inexperienced for him to take the risk. They'd have to wait until first light.

So Joe sat up and waited while the others slept. He planned on getting everyone up and breaking camp at dawn. He hadn't planned on opening the tent to half a foot of snow! Half an hour ago there had only been an inch or two.

There was no way they'd be able to make the descent in this. Swearing under his breath, he ordered all the boys to get dressed in as many layers of clothing as they had. "Two or three loose layers are warmer than one tight layer. And then wrap flannel shirts around your heads," he ordered, before tossing a plastic garbage bag at each of them. "Then rip those open and tie it around your head like this." He used Sinatra as an example. "Stay here while I go get the girls."

The snow was coming down so hard it was difficult to see more than a few inches ahead. Heading for the girls' tent, Joe found Prudence had already gotten the girls up and dressed. She held a cell phone in her hand. "I can't get a signal."

"Even if you could, there's no way anyone could come rescue us in this weather. Did you have the girls put on several layers of clothes?" At her nod, he said, "Good. Do you have anything you can tie over your heads? Hats or scarves or extra shirts? Put them on, fast. And if you don't have gloves, use extra socks on your hands. We've got to find some more permanent shelter as quickly as possible." Joe yanked the map out of his field jacket pocket and jabbed a finger at it. "According to this, there's a cabin not far from here."

"Is it time to use that survival stuff you told us about?" Keishon asked.

"Affirmative," Joe replied.

"Do you know no two snowflakes are the same?" Rosa said, entranced rather than afraid of the snowfall. "The number of combinations are infinite."

Joe knew one thing that wasn't infinite—his ability to get them to safety.

The next two hours were the longest in his life. Only his years of training kept him moving forward as if he was utterly confident of their ultimate location. The snow had obliterated the surrounding terrain, making familiar landmarks look utterly foreign.

Then he saw it...the bright red metal roof of a cabin.

Chapter Five

Prudence had never been so cold in her entire life. The fierce wind turned the snow into icy pellets that assaulted her face with stinging frequency. Her eyes were watering as a result of the unforgiving gusts of wind buffeting them. She was blindly following Joe, who was at the front of their group while she brought up the rear to make sure none of the kids in between got off track. The visibility was now so poor that they all had to hold hands in a human chain.

The snow was accumulating in drifts that went well beyond the tops of their hiking boots. Frostbite was a real concern—none of them were dressed for a surprise late-spring blizzard. They needed to find shelter immediately.

And if anyone could do that, Joe Wilder could. She had complete faith in his abilities. Marines were great at inspiring confidence and Joe was no exception.

It wasn't until Prudence bumped into Rosa's back

that she realized the group had come to a stop. A second later, she saw it—a cabin.

Thank heavens. Prudence wiped away a tear of relief before it froze on her numbed cheeks. Her legs were trembling from the energy required to trudge through the heavy layer of snow.

Inside the cabin, the relief from the bitterly stinging wind was immediate. As the storm howled outside, she quickly took stock of her surroundings. Their new home was basically one large room with a huge stone fireplace directly to her right. Two folding chairs leaned a little drunkenly near the hearth.

Straight ahead, against the back wall, there was an old-fashioned metal sink and a red hand-operated pump presumably to pump the water from a well. Shelves nailed to the wall above held a few rows of cans. In the opposite corner an open door led to a rudimentary toilet.

The place was dusty, but critter free as far as she could tell. At least on first sight. She'd have to thoroughly check it for spiders later. It was hardly the Ritz, but in their hour of need it appeared that way to her.

"While I start a fire, you kids get those wet boots and socks off," Joe ordered, heading for the small jar of matches perched on the mantel. "Prudence, check their feet for frostbite."

"I hate ssss...snow," Keishon wailed. "I've never been sss...sooo cold in my life." Her chattering teeth made her stutter.

Leaning down, Joe made fast work of starting a fire, using the pages from the notebook journal Prudence had given him as kindling before adding some of the larger logs stored beside the hearth. He'd noticed there was a sizable woodpile outside, covered with a blue tarp so they should be in good shape, providing the chimney wasn't clogged up. It wasn't. Finally something was going right.

Turning, Joe methodically checked the remaining VCRs' feet to make sure there was no sign of frostbite. He inspected Gem and Sinatra's fingers and toes. They were lucky. Only early stages, which were manageable. Nothing horrible. Something else going right.

The cabin was cold enough that you could see your breath, but the fire would warm things up. That was the first order of business. To get them warm.

As for him, the chill gripping his body had nothing to do with the outside temperature. If Joe thought being stuck in the tent with the VCRs was tough, that was nothing compared to the inner panic he was experiencing now.

Where before he'd just been along for the ride, so to speak, now he was responsible for the group's safety in a very real, very immediate way.

The morning was spent getting everyone warm and eating granola bars for a late breakfast. Joe and Sinatra were in charge of getting rid of cobwebs and spiders.

Prudence's muffled shriek from the far side of the cabin sent Joe racing to her side, his arms cradling her as she practically threw herself at him.

"What's wrong?" he demanded, his defenses on high alert as he rapidly searched the room for something that could have frightened her so badly. All he saw was a spider heading out the crack beneath the front door.

Shuddering, she whispered, "I'm sorry. It's just that I'm not fond of spiders. I'm fine now." Quickly pulling away from him, she smoothed her hair away from her face and recovered her usual confident demeanor so the kids wouldn't know she was spooked.

But it took Joe some time to recover from the feel of her clinging to him like seaweed.

After Prudence found an old-fashioned straw broom and swept the floor, they unpacked and spread their sleeping mats and sleeping bags in front of the fireplace in a semicircle.

"Are you using your Marine techniques to size up the situation, sir?" Sinatra quietly asked Joe.

Joe had already run through the entire gambit—there was enough firewood to last them maybe forty-eight hours, enough food for that long if they were careful. After several attempts, he'd finally gotten more than murky brown water to come out of the pump. If they boiled the water over the fire, it should be okay for drinking.

But there were so many unknowns—the length of the storm, the reliability of the fireplace, the possibility that one of the kids might get sick after their exposure to the cold. When he'd shivered his way through Winter Survival School with the Marines, the topic of protecting kids had never come up.

Not kids, he hastily reminded himself. Vertically challenged recruits.

Ah, hell, who was he kidding? One look at Rosa's trembling chin as she asked if they were going to die was worse than a sucker punch in the stomach.

"No one's dying on my watch," Joe fiercely declared, his jaw clenching with emotion.

"That's right," Prudence agreed. "We're going to be fine. So stop worrying, sweetie." Prudence gave Rosa a reassuring hug. "We'll be okay."

"We don't even have to call in the Marines," Sinatra said, gazing at Joe with absolute trust. "We've got our own Marine here to help us. He got us to this cabin, didn't he?"

For some reason, Sinatra's utter confidence in Joe hit him as hard as Rosa's fear.

"You'd think if someone built a cabin up here, they'd have neat stuff in it like big-screen TV and a VCR," Pete noted, wiggling his cold toes in front of the fireplace.

Of course, to Joe's way of thinking he already had a VCR—five of them to be exact. Five vertically challenged recruits. And now he was stuck with them. In a freak snowstorm.

Okay, this scenario stunk. But he could do this. He'd been in worse situations.

Yeah, but none of them had given him this sick feeling in the pit of his stomach.

"This isn't a resort hotel," Joe growled. "This is a rangers' cabin meant for emergency use. I'm going to go out and get some more firewood."

Stomping his way through the snow, Joe kicked the drifts out of his way. The heat of his anger should have been enough to melt the four-foot drifts. And that anger was directed at himself.

He'd had a bad feeling about the weather yesterday morning. He should have acted on that feeling. Should have trusted his gut. Should have called an early halt to this ridiculous wilderness adventure and sent them all home.

Then those kids would be home in their own bed tonight, safe and warm.

Regrets. God, he was an expert about regrets, about *if only's*. If only he'd been on that helo, he might have been able to do something to prevent the accident that had killed three of his fellow Marines. *If only, if only, if only.* The words beat into his brain like a drum that wouldn't stop.

Gritting his teeth, Joe picked up the logs one by one, until his arms were full. Even then he was in no hurry to go back inside. But there was no sense in risking further damage to his already mildly frostbitten fingers.

There was also no sense hiding outside. The guilt was inside of him and there was no running away from it. It was as much a part of him as his cold-numbed face and his disillusioned eyes. There was no escaping it.

"This cabin is even better than our tents," Sinatra said that evening as they all sat around the fireplace, carefully roasting the six squashed marshmallows that Prudence had found in a Baggie at the bottom of her backpack.

"At least it's got a john," Gem acknowledged.

"A head," Sinatra reminded him. "In the Marines they call it a head."

"I'm not in the Marines," Gem said.

"What if they don't find us and the food runs out and we have to eat someone?" Pete asked out of the blue.

"That's not going to happen," Prudence assured them.

"And if it did we'd eat you first, because you're the fattest one," Keishon said irritably.

"I'm not fat!" Pete shouted. "And I thought you were a vegetarian."

"For you I might make an exception," Keishon sniffed.

"You're a bloodthirsty bunch," Joe growled, the pounding in his head made worse by their arguing.

"Talking of bloodthirsty, let's tell ghost stories around the fire. I'll go first," Pete declared.

"I think it should be a round-robin story, with each person telling a part of the story," Rosa stated and the others agreed. "But you can still go first," she graciously told Pete.

"It started in this very cabin," Pete said in a dramatic voice. "Aliens landed one night and caught a bunch of campers, sucking the life out of them until they were dead. Ever since then, they've haunted this cabin."

"The aliens?" Keishon asked.

"No, the dead campers," Pete replied in exasperation. "They've haunted this cabin—"

"Why?" Rosa interrupted him to ask. "Why this cabin? Why don't they just roam the mountainside where they were camping? It would make more sense if you had them killed here in the cabin and not just haunting here."

"Fine." Pete's face reflected his irritation even as he took her editorial suggestions. "I'll start again. The family was staying in this very cabin when there was a strange light outside the window."

As if on cue, there was a flash of light outside, making all the kids shriek.

"Thunder snow," Joe explained, from his position near the window.

Prudence noticed that Joe had stayed there near the window and the entrance as if he were on guard duty. He'd grown increasingly tense all day. She meant to ask him about that as soon as the kids were asleep. If there was something about their situation Joe wasn't telling her, then she needed to know what it was. Seemingly they weren't in any danger now that they'd found shelter. They had food and water and heat. Even so, Joe had not relaxed his defensive stance.

"That wasn't thunder snow, it was aliens," Pete maintained, really getting into his story now. "And they waited until the family was asleep before sneaking inside and attacking them, sucking the life from them."

"Okay, my turn," Rosa declared. "It looked like the aliens were sucking the life from the family but it was really only their way of checking out who they were. The aliens didn't kill them, they just did an ultrafast medical checkup on them and discovered how old each one was, that sort of stuff. But then the family woke up and..."

"My turn," Sinatra said. "The family woke up and used their digital camera to take photos of the aliens and put those photos on the Internet using their palm held computer. The aliens had better computers, and could beam them right up into their spaceship."

"But when they beamed them up, they killed them," Pete inserted.

"You already had your turn," Rosa reminded him.

"The aliens showed the family how to improve communications," Sinatra continued, "and how to make their computers work just by thinking something. And then they..."

"My turn," Keishon said. "And then they told them that they had to be good to animals and not eat meat."

"What kind of weeny alien would say that?" Pete demanded in outrage. "There's no way that would ever happen!"

"My turn," Gem said. "And when they were beamed back to earth, the family realized that they'd picked up a terrible skin-eating alien disease."

"Now we're talking." Pete's voice reflected his approval, as did his high-five with Gem. "Skin-eating alien disease. Nice one!"

"It started at their toes and traveled up their legs," Gem said.

"And the family was sure it was going to die, when they were suddenly surprised by a boy-wizard who came down the fireplace," Rosa inserted.

Pete rolled his eyes at her. "Santa Claus comes down the fireplace, not Harry Potter."

"He's my wizard and I can have him do whatever he wants," Rosa firmly maintained. "With a wave of his magical wand, he cures the alien disease."

"Aliens are stronger than wizards," Pete maintained.

A heated discussion followed on that topic until Gem pointed out, "We had aliens and wizards but no ghosts. Maybe we should start another story."

"Fine. I'll go first," Pete quickly said. "It started here in this very cabin. The family sleeping here…"

"You can't tell that same story," Rosa told him. "You have to start again."

"This isn't the same story," Pete denied. "This time the flash outside was caused by a ghost, not an alien."

"I read a library book about ghost stories, you know," Rosa said. "One had a big black dog who attacked anyone who came near. They could hear it bark and growl, but they couldn't see it."

"Probably because the barking and growling came

from an audiocassette," the ever-practical Sinatra said. "Sound effects, nothing more than sound effects."

"The odds of aliens from other planets is higher than that ghosts really exist," said the mathematically inclined Rosa. "Don't you think so, Sergeant?"

Joe might not know about aliens and ghosts, but he sure knew about being haunted. And he was definitely feeling haunted at the moment. Haunted by being yet again responsible for a mission that had gone wrong.

As everyone else settled in their sleeping bags, Joe hunkered down in front of the fireplace—feeding the fire with the logs he'd brought in and feeding his inner turmoil with memories.

Guilt weighed on him heavily as he made his way back to his position near the door. It was colder here, but he didn't feel the chill. He'd given up hope of ever really feeling warm inside again.

Well, that wasn't exactly true. He'd given up hope of feeling at peace, but Prudence certainly did manage to make him feel warm inside. Very warm. Which was very stupid.

His commanding officer's daughter was the one woman who was off-limits to him.

But that realization didn't seem to stop the volatile chemistry between them from increasing. Not that being snowbound in a two-room cabin with five pre-adolescent VCRs was exactly a romantic setup.

Last night, when he'd walked out of his tent and found Prudence, he'd definitely felt a connection with her. A reluctant connection to be sure but it was there, despite his attempts to make it disappear.

Even now, he was aware of her as she tossed and turned in her sleeping bag. He heard her every sigh, felt her every move. She was driving him crazy.

When she suddenly jackknifed into a sitting position, he quietly growled, "Can't you sit still for ten minutes?" She'd been bustling around the cabin all evening, fussing over her students, hovering over the large pot hanging above the fire as she made dinner from the food they'd brought with them supplemented by some cans of spaghetti stored in the cabin. How could he have known that he'd find her Suzie Homemaker routine incredibly sexy? "You're going to wake up the…uh…your students."

"I'm sorry, I…" The sound of her stomach growling interrupted her words. She blushed. He hadn't seen a woman blush in ages.

"Here," he said gruffly. "Eat this." He handed her an apple from his ALICE.

"You were supposed to eat that last night," she said in an accusatory voice. Because of the heavy weather, they'd had beef jerky, trail mix and apples for dinner last night. "You need to eat it."

"Just take the apple. I saw the way you gave your helping to your students instead of taking enough food for yourself."

"You did the same thing," she replied, leaving her sleeping bag behind to pad over in her woolen socks to join him in the shadowy far corner of the cabin. He was sitting on one of the folding chairs. She carefully moved the other chair closer to him so that the kids wouldn't hear them talking. Outside, the storm continued. Gusts of wind rattled the windows, making her grateful that they weren't out there facing Mother Nature's wrath unprotected. Prudence was protected, not just by the cabin's walls and the warmth of the fire, but by Joe Wilder's presence. "The least you could do would be to eat the apple since you didn't have much of anything else.''

''Just take the apple and stop arguing.''

She eyed the apple before raising her eyes to meet his gaze. He really did have the most incredible eyes. They seemed to see clear into her soul. ''I'll split it with you.''

''I'm a Marine, ma'am, I don't need much food.''

''I'm sure you chew nails for breakfast, Sergeant. And you can call me Prudence instead of ma'am. You said my name before.'' At his slightly startled look, she added, ''This morning when we first arrived at the cabin.'' Taking the apple he still held out, she pulled a Swiss Army knife from her backpack and sliced the apple in half. ''I cut, so you get to choose.''

''Choose what?''

''Which piece of apple you want.'' She held out both her hands, each holding a portion of the apple.

''I already told you...''

''That you're superhuman and don't require food like the rest of the human race,'' she completed for him with a teasing grin. ''I know, I know. Come on, just take the apple.''

''Said Eve to Adam,'' Joe muttered.

She raised a teasing eyebrow at him before asking, ''Do you think I'm trying to tempt you, Sergeant?''

''If you are, then the least you can do is call me Joe,'' he drawled, taking the smaller piece of apple.

''I wouldn't dream of trying to tempt a Marine,'' she assured him.

''Why not? Think you couldn't do it? Don't sell yourself short.'' His voice was gruff.

His words surprised her. She still had her black thermal leggings on as well as a long T-shirt and flannel shirt that almost went down to her knees. Not exactly a seductive outfit. Maybe he just couldn't see her. She and Joe were both in the sheltering shadows where the fireglow gave way to the darkness. "Is that a compliment of sorts?"

"Affirmative."

So he thought she could tempt him, hmm? Interesting. Prudence finished munching the last of the apple before speaking. "Then let me return the compliment by saying that I'm grateful for the great work you did in getting us to this cabin."

His soft laugh was bitter. "If I'd been doing my job, you'd all be snug in your own beds tonight instead of up here on this mountain in the middle of a blizzard."

She frowned at him as another gust rattled the window nearby. "What makes you say that?"

"It's the truth."

Or his version of it. "Look, you had no way of knowing this blizzard would hit. I listened to the weather forecast. They didn't say anything about that storm coming ashore."

"I didn't like the look of the weather this morning," Joe said, glaring at the darkness outside as snow piled up against the bottom of the windowpane.

"Did you know that a blizzard was coming?"

Joe waved her words away with an angry slash of his hand. "You don't understand. You all could have died on my watch. If we hadn't found the cabin in time, if one of you had twisted an ankle or broken a leg, if you'd suffered from hypothermia or frostbite—" He broke off, his voice was thick with emotion. For the first time his control showed signs of slipping.

Prudence put her hand on his arm. His muscles were

hard and tense. "But none of those things happened," she softly reassured him. "No one is going to die on your watch."

He turned to glare at her and the cold fury in his blue eyes scorched her as he yanked his arm away. "You think it hasn't happened before? It has. Three Marines are dead and it happened on my watch. Three families lost their son, their husband, their father. *On...my...watch.*" He said each word distinctly, bitterly, hopelessly. As if they were individual bullets searing his soul.

She could see the pain in his eyes, there beneath the anger. Then a shutter came down, shutting her out. "There was a helo accident a few weeks ago." His expression was now blank, his voice military crisp, completely lacking the emotion of a moment ago. "We were finishing up a routine overseas op and I was the training officer in charge. There was another sergeant there, he asked if he could swap training missions with me. I did the scheduling, it was my call. I gave the okay. It was just a training mission, no big deal. The Cobra took off, then something went wrong. It suddenly lost power and crashed. There were no survivors. And it all happened on my watch."

Prudence was deeply touched by his pain, even if he was making heroic efforts to hide it from her. She knew it couldn't have been easy confiding in her. "I'm so sorry." She touched his hand. He didn't pull away this time, so she quietly continued. "I can understand how you might feel guilty, but the accident wasn't your fault."

Joe silently cursed his loose tongue even as he stood and moved away from her. What the hell had he been thinking of, confiding in her, letting her get close to him? He needed his head examined. And if that happened, if any whiff of emotional problems or instability went on his record then his life as a Marine might well be over.

Joe loved the Marine Corps. He came from a large military family, all of whom were rough, tough, can't-get-enough United States Marines. He'd never had trouble coping with anything in his entire life. Until now.

Now everything he valued most was at risk.

He had to protect himself. He had to put her at arm's length once more. "*You* understand?" His voice, his very demeanor mocked her. "I doubt that. What could a cautious daddy's girl like you possibly know about guilt?"

"I know plenty," Prudence quietly replied. "When I was a teenager, I almost killed my mom."

Chapter Six

"What are you talking about?" Joe demanded, taken aback by her words.

"I just told you," Prudence said, her gaze shifting away from his.

"That as a teenager you almost killed your mom?" he repeated in disbelief. "How? By driving her crazy with your stubbornness?" he scoffed.

"No, by driving recklessly and getting involved in a serious car accident." Her voice vibrated with anger at his mocking attitude. "My mother broke her pelvis and was in the hospital and in physical therapy for weeks. So, yes, I do know all about guilt."

"I'm sorry," he said quietly. "I had no idea."

"You've got that right." She ran a weary hand through her hair, tucking it behind her ears to get it away from her face. Lifting her chin, she gave him a challenging stare that dared him to turn away from her. "You had no idea, yet you still assumed that I didn't know what I was talking about, that you were the only one who'd ever experienced survival guilt.''

"I apologize," he said quietly, facing her look without flinching. "But your situation isn't the same. Your mother didn't die. She recovered."

"And I thank God for that every day. But it doesn't lessen the fact that I brought her a great deal of physical pain. Did I do it deliberately? No. Did you do anything that caused that crash? Were the mechanics working on it? Did you deliberately avoid getting on that helicopter because you knew it would crash? No, no and no."

A muscle jerked in his jaw. "That doesn't change the fact that if I'd been doing my job, you'd all be home safe in your own beds tonight."

She blinked at him. "How did we jump from the helicopter crash to this spring blizzard? I don't get the connection. I must not have gotten the memo saying you were in charge of the entire world," she noted with mocking humor.

"Not the entire world. Just my corner of it."

"What about me?" she countered. "I could just as well be saying that if I'd been doing my job, then I wouldn't have allowed my students to get in this mess. After all, this weekend trip was my idea in the first place."

Joe raised a dark eyebrow at her. "Are we going to argue about who should feel guilty about this mess?" he inquired wryly.

"Why not? We argue about practically everything else."

"I'm not usually the argumentative type," Joe said.

"Neither am I," she admitted.

"I wonder what it is about our...chemistry together that makes us argue so much?"

"We don't argue *all* the time."

"Now you're arguing about how much we argue," Joe noted with a slow smile.

Grinning, she nudged him with her elbow. "Am not."

"Are, too," he retorted in kind, nudging her right back.

"Now we're sounding like Pete and Keishon." She nodded her head toward the fireplace where the kids were sound asleep in their individual sleeping bags.

Joe's gaze followed hers. "I think Pete's got a case of puppy love going on there and that's why he argues with her."

"Is that why you argue with me?" The words were out of her mouth before she could stop them.

"No, ma'am," Joe said solemnly, his blue eyes gleaming with humor in the shadows as he turned to look directly at her. "I only argue with you when you're wrong."

"Funny," she murmured, nudging him again with her elbow. "That's the only time I argue with you, too."

"Besides, my puppy love days are long gone," he added.

"Mine, too," she agreed.

"Who did you have a crush on when you were their age?"

"Bobby Wills," she immediately replied. "How about you?"

"No, I never had a crush on Bobby Wills."

She laughed. She had the feeling that, in the past, Joe was the kind of man who made a lot of women laugh. He'd probably made more than his fair share cry, too. Maybe not. Maybe she was judging him by an inaccurate yardstick, one thrown off-kilter by her experience with Steven Banks. There was certainly more to Joe than merely a gung ho Marine.

He was another tortured soul. Maybe that's why she'd felt such a connection with him. She knew what he was going through, even if he doubted that she understood. She knew how guilt could eat you up and tear your heart out.

She wondered what the connection was between his reaction to the kids and the helicopter crash. Was it simply being responsible for them, as he'd been responsible for the men on his watch? Or was there more?

What had they been talking about before he'd cracked her up with his droll comment? Oh, yes. Puppy love. "I'll bet you can't even remember the name of the first girl you had a crush on," Prudence challenged him. "I mean, there have probably been so many girls."

"Her name was Betsy Wiseapple and she had red hair, freckles and braces."

"You're making that up."

"A Marine never makes things up," he solemnly replied.

"I should know that," she said, turning to look at him.

Joe turned at the same time. His lips were now only a few inches away from hers. "Yes, you should."

Prudence should also do the cautious thing and move away. Ever since her rebellious teenage years, Prudence had tried to stay on the straight and narrow and do the right thing to make up for her former wild behavior.

But sharing confidences with Joe in the shadowy darkness was tempting her to stop being prudent.

Slowly leaning toward her, Joe gave her every chance to pull away. Instead she watched as he came closer.

At the first touch of his lips against hers, something inside of her melted. Her heart gave a strange little leap as she tasted the sweetness of the apple they'd just shared on his warm lips.

His kiss was surprisingly hesitant, which both shocked and delighted her.

He wasn't sweeping her off her feet as if she were one of the many women he'd no doubt charmed in the past. This was different. He wasn't storming her defenses, he was gently seducing them. His mouth brushed across hers with slow and reverent strokes, each gentle exploration creating a new sense of expectancy.

Gradually increasing the pressure, the kiss lost all tentativeness and blossomed as he coaxed her lips to not only cling to his but to part, allowing him the liberty of dipping his tongue into the warm depths of her mouth.

It certainly wasn't the first time Prudence had ever been kissed this way, but it was certainly the first time she'd ever responded this way. She'd secretly never understood the appeal of French kissing until this very moment. Now, as he teased her with the tip of his tongue, she shivered with unspoken delight.

She could easily get addicted to this. She'd waited all her life for this.

Parting her lips even more, she murmured with pleasure as Joe tasted her, his tongue swirling, probing and exploring as if she were some incredible delicacy that he couldn't get enough of.

The sudden sound of a sleepy murmur startled her. Quickly breaking off their kiss, Prudence scooted away from Joe, almost falling off her chair. Silently berating herself for her momentary lapse in cautious judgment, Prudence returned to the fire and comforted a restless Rosa until the girl fell back into a deep sleep.

But Joe remained in the shadows, as if he didn't think he was worthy of coming into the light and the warmth.

The next morning the worst of the storm had broken. Snow blanketed everything, making rocky outcroppings indistinguishable from drifts. The temperature rose above freezing and some of the snow began melting.

By noon the sky had cleared enough for a watered-down stream of sunlight to peek through. Joe spent every moment preparing for their rescue.

Just a little longer, he kept telling himself as he hacked branches from a few of the snow-covered evergreens that stood like majestic sentinels. Just a little longer...

"You're not supposed to chop down trees in a national park," Keishon yelled at him from the cabin's covered front porch. "Sir," she added as he ducked to avoid having a pile of melting snow dumped on his head from one of the higher branches.

"I'm not chopping down trees," Joe replied, brushing wet snow from his face. "Just a few branches."

"This land belongs to everyone," Keishon primly

reminded him. "So we should be careful not to damage it."

"I'm not damaging it."

"I don't think that tree would agree with you," Keishon declared. "You shouldn't be chopping off branches. You're going to get into trouble."

Too late. Joe was already in trouble.

"What are you doing?" Keishon yelled again.

Yeah, that was the question all right. What the heck was Joe doing—kissing his commanding officer's daughter the way he had last night? He shouldn't have been kissing her any which way, but certainly not as if she was his last hope of salvation on earth.

"You better get back inside," Joe ordered Keishon. "It's too cold out here."

"You're out here, sir."

"Because I'm trained to do this."

"To cut down branches?" she asked doubtfully.

"To make sure we get rescued today." That's what Joe was hanging on to. With the clearing weather, a helicopter should be able to start the search. He had no doubt that Prudence's father would make sure that a search party was started as soon as possible. And chances were they'd search in all the likely places first, like this deserted ranger's cabin.

But just to be sure, Joe laid the dark green boughs out in the pristine white snow so that they formed a huge X. This way a rescue helicopter would be sure to find them. And the sooner that happened the better as far as Joe was concerned.

His orders were to take care of Prudence. That meant getting her off this mountain and away from him. He was no good to any woman in the shape he was in. And he was certainly no good to the one woman who was off-limits to him.

The helicopter arrived later that afternoon. Joe was waiting on the front porch, gathering more firewood. He heard the whirring sounds as the helo came closer. For one moment, as the sun bounced off the metal rotor blades, he was thrown back to that moment six weeks ago when he'd stood watching another chopper.

Joe swore, low and harsh, cursing the memories that wouldn't disappear. He fought down the rising emotion, fearing that if he let it out it would consume him.

Narrowing his eyes, Joe shifted his gaze to Prudence who'd just joined him on the porch. He should never have confessed as much as he had to her last night. Survivor guilt—a neat and tidy name for a gritty and messy emotion.

Running out into the snow, Joe waved his hands, indicating the best landing place. The snow had melted in a relatively flat area. The hovering helo softly touched down there a few moments later.

"Sergeant Wilder?" the copilot asked as he jumped out, bending low to avoid the downdraft.

"Affirmative," Joe replied.

"Any injuries?"

"Negative."

"There's more bad weather moving in, Sergeant," the copilot said. "So the faster we can get this rescue mission accomplished the better."

Joe nodded his agreement before rushing back to the cabin. Prudence was gathering their backpacks onto the porch but Joe stopped her. "We need to move everyone out ASAP. Forget the backpacks, just get in the helicopter." Since the snow was still up to his knees near the shadowy front of the cabin, he simply picked up Rosa and headed out to the helo, handing her over to the copilot who helped the girl inside the passenger compartment.

Joe returned for the other students until all were aboard the helo. Joe then turned back for Prudence, but the copilot stopped him with a hand on his arm. "That's all we can carry this trip, Sergeant. We'll be back for you two."

"You don't understand," Joe barked. "That's Sergeant Major Martin's daughter. You have to take her. *Now*."

"I don't care if she's the First Lady," the copilot, clearly not a Marine, replied. "We're packed as much as possible. Putting anyone else on board would put us all at risk. Just sit tight, Sergeant. We'll be back as soon as we can." He hopped into the helicopter and shut the door.

Joe ducked and hurriedly moved away as the rotors turned to full power and the helicopter took off. He closed his eyes rather than shield them against the blast caused by the helicopter's downdraft. Loose snow flew in his face, mocking him. Just when he thought he was out of the woods, things got worse.

Sure, he'd gotten rid of the VCRs. But now he was snowbound in an isolated cabin in the mountains with a woman whose kiss packed the punch of a 40 mm grenade launcher.

Not for long, he reminded himself. Not for long.

"They'll be back." Joe shouted the reassurance to Prudence. He repeated it even louder this time. "They'll be back!"

"And do you plan on standing out there waiting for

them?'' she asked as if she knew why he was keeping his distance.

Was she laughing at him? No one laughed at a Marine. She should know better, after having been raised by the Sergeant Major. ''No, I don't plan on standing out here waiting,'' he replied, stomping onto the porch and brushing the snow off. Too bad he didn't have any arctic gear with him. But then who could have known that the weather in North Carolina in early May would get so temperamental?

No wonder they referred to Mother Nature and not Father Nature. Only a female would be this unpredictable and recalcitrant.

''I was just making soup when the helicopter arrived,'' Prudence said as she ushered him back into the cabin. ''Want some? It's just instant chicken noodle.''

''I'm not hungry,'' he lied, his stomach growling in protest. He'd skipped breakfast so that Prudence and the kids would have more food. While there were several cans of baked beans and pasta in the cabin, the preadolescents had a bottomless appetite.

''I can't possibly eat all this by myself,'' she protested. ''It'll go to waste otherwise. Besides I could use some help getting the place back in order before they return for us.''

Us. What was she doing referring to them as an us? Just because he'd kissed her last night, that didn't mean there was an *us* here.

Prudence knew Joe had been avoiding her all morning. And she'd let him. Her own thoughts were still too jumbled to sort out logically.

Being alone with him in the cabin was infinitely different than having her students there. The very air seemed to vibrate. Something was happening between them, had already happened when he'd kissed her last night. And now she was still struggling to come to terms with what it all meant.

Did he regret kissing her? Did she regret kissing him? Logically she might, but in her heart there was no contrition at her incautious behavior. Being kissed by him had simply felt too good, too right.

Which was a very dangerous thing. Joe Wilder was a man who knew how to treat women, knew how to seduce them, definitely knew how to kiss them. It didn't necessarily mean anything and she'd do well to remember that.

She and Joe ate their soup in silence and then began cleaning up. Neatness was a requirement in the Marine Corps. It had become second nature to her and she suspected to Joe as well. They worked well together, until he turned and bumped into her.

His hands automatically came out to hold her upright. In an instant, awareness flared, making her want him with a hunger and desperation that shocked her. And intrigued her.

Their gazes met and held. Shivers danced down her spine. She wasn't cold, however. No, she was definitely warm and getting hotter by the minute. All because of the way he was looking at her. His blue eyes searched her face, lingering on her lips in a way that told her he was thinking about that kiss last night. His gaze caressed what his mouth and hands could not.

Then the man became the Marine once again as he stepped away from her. Heading to the window, he looked outside. "That rescue team should have been back by now," Joe muttered.

Prudence shrugged. "Maybe they had others they

had to rescue. We're probably not the only ones caught unprepared by this blizzard.''

Caught unprepared. A cardinal sin for a Marine.

Stepping outside, Joe scanned the sky and swore. The wind had picked up while they'd been inside and dark storm clouds were billowing to their west, moving in fast. It looked like the bad weather the copilot had told him about was moving in faster than expected.

Fifteen minutes later it was snowing heavily again. As Joe feared, the storm wasn't over yet. They wouldn't be going anyplace today…or tonight, either, for that matter.

Chapter Seven

"What should we dine on this evening?" Prudence inquired in her best pseudohaughty maître d' voice. "We have a lovely selection of pasta on the menu. Would you prefer canned spaghetti or canned ravioli?"

"I'd prefer to get off this mountain," Joe growled, pacing the floor like a caged tiger.

"Anyone ever tell you that you can be quite crabby?" she inquired as she attempted to use a manual can opener on the ravioli.

He appeared a bit affronted by her comment. "If you think I'm crabby you should meet my friend Curt. He's always been the crabby one. I'm the..."

"The what?" she prompted over her shoulder. "The charmer? The ladies' man?"

"What gives you that idea?" he demanded, whisking the can from her hands and using the stubborn can opener with ease.

"Probably your practiced routine when we first met."

"That was no routine," Joe replied, plunking the now-opened can onto the counter beside her. "I'll have you know that my routine is much better than that."

"And I'm sure it's usually successful with members of the opposite sex. Put a guy like you in Marine dress blues and there's really no contest, right? Women swoon at your feet."

He frowned at her. "What do you mean, a guy like me?"

"You don't need me to tell you that you're good-looking."

"But you're immune, right? Marines don't do anything for you."

"That's right." She wasn't lying. Marines hadn't done anything for her...until now.

"I would have thought that being raised as a Marine brat, you'd embrace the Corps values."

"Honor, courage, commitment. I believe in those, but I didn't and still don't believe that only Marines have those qualities. And I rebelled against the tight rein my father kept on me. Then there was the fact that we moved a lot, all over the U.S. and even overseas once. We were stationed in Okinawa when I was nine."

He gave her a startled look. "Really? My dad was stationed there, too. The whole family was with him."

"When was that?" Prudence asked.

When he gave her the date, she blinked at him in surprise. "That's when we were there."

"Along with several thousand others." Joe sat on

one of the folding chairs and balanced his plate of ravioli on his lap. The cabin had no table.

Sitting beside him on her own chair, she stared at him more closely. "Did you have a nickname?"

"Did you?" he countered.

"Yes, but I'm not telling you what it is."

"My brothers and I used to hang around with a girl we called Princess Pug," he noted almost absently.

Her strangled cough made Joe pause. "Are you okay?"

"Yes, I'm just stunned."

Narrowing his eyes, he gave her an intent look before shaking his head. "No way. You're not...you're not Princess Pug?"

She turned her profile to him. "You don't recognize the nose, Flyboy?"

"You had a cute little nose," he noted slowly, staring at her as if he couldn't believe what he was hearing. "That's why we gave you that nickname."

"Which I would never have tolerated from anyone else," she informed him. "But you and your brothers were very nice to the new kid on the block when I first moved there. It was the first overseas assignment I'd ever been on with my parents and I had trouble adjusting at first. I was scared and alone and you made me feel better. Then you were gone."

Joe nodded. "My dad's tour of duty was over and we headed back to the States."

"I never even knew your real name. You all went by nicknames. Flyboy, Ranger, Eagle and Champ. You were going to be a pilot."

"I changed my mind. You were going to be a princess."

"I changed my mind," she replied with a grin.

"It's a tight job market in the princess business, huh?"

She laughed and nodded. "Then there was the fact that I went to boarding school for a while, an all-girls high school, and met a real princess from a tiny European principality. She was so smooth and confident that I knew I'd never be able to compete. We ended up friends, though."

"You're still a princess in your father's eyes," Joe told her.

She just rolled her eyes.

"Princess Pug." He stared at her in amazement. "After all this time. Tell me more about what you were like as a teenager."

"Why?"

"Because I'm having a hard time picturing you as a wild rebel."

"Trust me," Prudence said. "I was wild. I didn't take orders from anyone."

"You still don't do that very well," he noted dryly. "At least not from me."

"I've tried very hard to become a more cautious person," she informed him.

"Since the car accident, you mean."

Prudence nodded and her expression turned serious. "I would have done anything to make up for what I did. The accident was my fault. That's a fact, not a feeling."

"Marines don't have feelings," Joe said.

"The few, the proud, the unfeeling?" she misquoted the recruiting line. "I don't think so."

"Marines must not fail."

"And you think you failed by not getting on that helicopter that crashed?" she said astutely.

Joe clenched his jaw. "You have no idea what I think."

"Then tell me."

"No." Just like that he ended their conversation and focused all his attention on his meal, which he consumed with quick efficiency.

She couldn't believe how he was able to turn his emotions on and off the way he did. And she couldn't believe that he was the Flyboy she'd known as a young girl. But it did explain the connection she'd felt with him.

Wow. Flyboy. After all this time.

They finished the dinner just as they had their lunch. In silence.

Great. She was really getting aggravated now. They'd just discovered a shared childhood past and the guy clammed up. Fine. Let him brood. She wasn't going to beg him to speak to her. She had bigger fish to fry.

Right after dinner, she set her plans into action and by the time Joe returned with a new batch of firewood she was just about ready.

"Since we're stuck here anyway, I'm taking a bath," Prudence announced. "While you've been pouting, I've been boiling water."

Pouting? Joe thought to himself, immediately defensive. There was no pouting in the United States Marine Corps.

Her accusation momentarily distracted him from the rest of her declaration. Her taking a bath. That would probably require her taking off her clothes. Definitely not a good idea. Besides, there was no hot water....

Which was why she'd been boiling water. The woman was serious. She was clearly out of her mind.

"Listen, princess, this isn't a health spa here. Take your bath when you get home."

It was as direct an order as he could possibly have given her, delivered in his best drill sergeant voice.

It had absolutely no effect on her. "I haven't had a bath in four days. This is not open for discussion, Sergeant. I am taking that bath. Look, I've used the clothesline to string up this blanket I found to provide some privacy. I've been planning this all afternoon. Ever since I realized that helicopter wasn't coming back for us today."

Here he'd been having a heart attack worrying about their rescue and she'd been planning her *bath?*

He had to get out of there. She was driving him crazy. After discovering they'd hung out together as kids on Okinawa, they'd spent the evening in silence. Or to be more precise, after she'd tried to get him to talk about the helicopter crash he'd been silent and she'd attempted to start several conversations. But he wasn't having any part of that. And he sure as heck wasn't standing still for this bath idea.

Which meant he had to move on or move out.

Only problem was that they already had enough firewood piled up on the hearth to last them a year or two. He could go out to take a walk, but it was colder than a dead snake out there.

He was getting soft in his old age. No, quite the opposite. He was getting hard. And it was all because of her, the woman stripping behind that sorry excuse for a blanket, the one that was so threadbare he could see her shadowy outline clearly.

It was like some kind of kinky shadow theater, where he could only see her silhouette as she carefully bent over to test the temperature of the bath water in the old metal tub she'd found. Her breasts were high and firm, her bottom lush and round. His mouth went dry, his throat constricted as desire hit him with the force of a blow.

She'd pinned her hair on top of her head. Her slender arms reached for the edge of the tub. Her long leg lifted, her toes pointed as she daintily stepped into the tub. She was killing him here.

The tub wasn't big enough for her to lie in, so she knelt, leaning over to pour the water over her shoulders.

"You're awfully quiet out there," she said. "Are you okay?"

"Affirmative," he said in a gravelly voice.

He really should look away. She clearly had no idea the kind of show she was putting on for him. The gentlemanly thing to do would be to turn his back, to walk away, to do anything but what he was doing.

But Joe could no more look away than he could stop breathing. In fact, he'd have better luck holding his breath, which he'd been doing since she'd first peeled off her shirt behind that screen of temptation otherwise known as a blanket.

He'd seen and done a lot over the years, but this shadow strip dance of hers was the most incredibly erotic thing he'd ever seen.

"Are you still there?" she called out.

"Affirmative." Joe's voice was getting downright hoarse now.

"What are you doing?"

"Nothing," he croaked.

"That doesn't sound like you. You're always doing something, never sitting still."

He was doing something, all right. He was acting

like a Peeping Tom. He should be ashamed of himself. He snapped his eyes shut.

What if she fell? What if she slipped in the tub and he was sitting here with his eyes closed?

Joe's eyes snapped open. He should keep an eye on her. Both eyes. Glued to her shapely form. She looked like a goddess. Who knew that the conservative clothes she wore hid such a gorgeous body?

Not that it mattered. Her gorgeous body didn't change the fact that she was still his commanding officer's daughter. Joe's orders were to keep her safe. Deciding how best to accomplish that goal was his duty.

That meant watching out for her. Surely there was no harm as long as he kept his hands to himself. And his lips. And his arms. And his fingertips.

Jeez, he had it bad. Thankfully his camouflage utility uniform was loose fitting because he'd just about be bursting his jeans right about now.

Restraint. A Marine prided himself on his restraint. Joe silently began reciting the Uniform Code of Military Justice. Nowhere in it did it say that it was legal for her to tempt him this way. Surely there had to be some law against it. If not there should be, because her body was definitely a lethal weapon—lethal to his self-control and peace of mind.

Prudence hadn't had the nightmare for years. She'd learned to wake herself up before things got too bad. But this time it crept up on her. She was driving the sporty red Miata her father had given her the year before on her sixteenth birthday. It was a glorious day, the sun was shining, Sting was singing through the outstanding sound system and her mother was complaining. Complaining that the music was too loud, that Prudence was driving too fast.

Prudence turned her head to tell her mother to lay off when it happened. So fast in real life, so slow in her nightmare. And there was nothing she could do.

Stop it! Stop it!

Joe heard her scream. He was beside her in an instant. She was still fighting the sleeping bag to get free and she almost socked him in the jaw with her frantic efforts.

"It's okay," he soothed her. "Prudence, it's okay. You were dreaming. It's okay. You're with me."

"Joe?"

"That's right." Cupping her face with his big hands, he wiped her tears away with his thumbs. "It's okay."

"I was dreaming about the car crash." Her voice was ragged, her breath coming in uneven spurts. "The one that hurt my mother."

"I won't say that it was just a nightmare because I know how bad they can feel." His voice was as soothing as his touch. He was stroking her cheek with his fingertips, slow, healing caresses.

The nightmare had felt bad, but his touch felt incredibly good. Closing her eyes, she swayed closer.

Lowering his hands to her shoulders, Joe drew Prudence near. She could feel his breath on her lips, could feel the thrum of his heart beneath her hands as they rested on his chest. The warmth of his body radiated through the cotton of his T-shirt.

Time froze, cocooning them in this moment without any thought of past or future. He cupped the curve of her jaw, his fingertips resting in the hollows behind her ear. Lowering his head, Joe touched his lips to hers, barely grazing them before leaning away to read the look on her face.

Her eyes fluttered open. He was so close yet not close enough. The sight of him filled her entire vision, leaving no room for anything else. She prayed he wouldn't stop, wouldn't push her away. Couldn't he see what he did to her?

And then his lips returned to hers to consume her mouth with a frenzy of need. She rejoiced at his passion, matching it.

Coaxing her lips to part even more, he probed the tender-veined flesh of her inner lip before coaxing her tongue to come play. His sweet boldness and pleasure-giving ways took her breath away.

While Joe's kiss transported her, his hands were working their own magic, sliding beneath her loose T-shirt to find her bare skin. Lowering her onto the partially opened sleeping bag, he blanketed her with his strong fully aroused male body.

She reached upward, sliding her arms around his waist. Cradled in his embrace, he was her insulation against all the nightmares, against the guilt and the pain. She was drowning in a sea of desire, offering herself to him in wanton invitation.

Her sensitized nerve endings vibrated with sheer pleasure as his hands moved beneath her T-shirt to cup her breasts. She'd discarded her bra before going to sleep, so there was nothing between them now. He brushed his thumb over the warm and willing peak, teasing it to attention.

Their frantic kiss continued, only broken off long enough for him to peel the shirt from her body. She took that opportunity to hook her fingers beneath the hem of his T-shirt and yank it over his head.

The firelight danced over them, bathing them in the heat of the flames. His eyes had never seemed so blue as he devoured her with his gaze.

The ripe lushness of her breasts thrust temptingly against his chest. She felt her nipples tingle as his mouth approached. When his lips closed around her and tugged softly into his mouth, she arched her back at the unbelievable burst of dark and sweet joy.

Combing her fingers through his hair she held on to him as her world spun completely out of control.

Just when she didn't think she could stand the pleasure a second later without exploding, he shifted his attention to her other breast and the wild ride of excitement began again.

Passion prevailed over caution as she explored his body with quick movements, using a butterfly-soft touch as if fearing he'd reject her advances. He did not. Instead he welcomed them, reveled in them, growling his pleasure as her fingertips brushed the coppery coins of his nipples.

His lips returned to hers, teaching her new moves, exploring every corner of her mouth and taking her deeper into the welcoming arms of desire. She was on fire with wanting him. Her body was tight with anticipation. He knew exactly where to touch her, how to bring her the most pleasure.

She felt her arms and limbs seeking to entangle themselves with his, silently cursing the bulky sleeping bag for coming between them.

Tearing his mouth from hers, Joe jackknifed into a sitting position. Prudence hazily thought he was going to free her from her sleeping bag so that she could wrap herself around him as she longed to do.

Instead he scrambled to his feet and hurriedly

stepped away from her. In a blink Joe was standing several feet away, his back ramrod straight, his demeanor that of a Marine standing at attention.

"I am not making love to my commanding officer's daughter," he barked, his voice bouncing off the cabin's walls. "He'd have me court-martialed!"

Chapter Eight

Prudence willed her hands not to shake as she hastily reached for her discarded T-shirt and yanked it back over her head. "I don't believe this." The words weren't meant to be spoken aloud but they were.

"Believe it," Joe stated gruffly. "And believe that what just happened between us can't happen again."

"Because of my father." Prudence laughed but there was no humor in it as she hugged her knees with a fierce determination not to cry. "Which is really ironic, considering that the last guy I was involved with was *only* interested in me because of my father. And now you *won't* get involved with me because of my father."

"What do you mean, the last guy was only interested in you because of your father?"

"He was a disgruntled Navy officer who wanted to pay back my father because my father had given him a less than glowing review during advance career developmental training. He figured seducing me and then dumping me would be a way to get to my father.''

Joe swore, the quiet curses rough with emotion. ''Did you love him?''

''I don't know. I thought I did.''

''I see. When we first met back at the base you seemed to have a grudge against Marines. But this guy was Navy.''

Her smile was bitter. ''Interservice rivalry raises its head again, huh? Trust me, I've had my share of Marine dates gone wrong as well. I didn't want to get involved with another military man.'' Unspoken but clearly communicated were the words *until now*.

''What we just shared, uh...'' Joe paused, cleared his throat and started again. ''You know when people share an intense experience like we've shared over the past few days, being snowbound up here and all. Well, it affects the emotions in an artificial way.''

''There is absolutely nothing artificial about my aggravation with you,'' Prudence shot back, anger momentarily superseding the embarrassed misery.

Where did he get off talking to her as if she were one of her own students? Telling her that her emotions weren't real. They were real all right. False emotions wouldn't be this painful. The bruised roots of her self-esteem felt as if they'd been yanked out of the ground and stomped on.

''Being aggravated with me is good.'' He sounded relieved and that made her feel like crawling under a rock.

''Being aggravated with you is good, but wanting to kiss you is bad. Got it,'' she said curtly, refusing to look directly at him and addressing her words to a spot somewhere beyond his head. What an idiot she'd been. "Don't worry, I can take the hint."

"No, that's not it..."

But she wasn't listening any longer. The pain was becoming too intense, and the need to hide it from him was taking all her self-discipline.

Despite the fact that Prudence confessed her own feelings of guilt about her mother's injuries, despite the fact that she discovered he'd been the boy who'd been kind to her all those years ago in Okinawa, Joe still didn't see her. Not for who she was. In his eyes, she was just his commanding officer's daughter. Nothing more.

Even now, after almost making love to her, he still didn't see her as Prudence the *woman*.

And that hurt. Immensely.

But she had her pride. She wasn't going to let him see what havoc he'd wrought on her emotions. She wasn't going to let him see her period.

"I'm going back to sleep," she declared, slipping down into her sleeping bag and yanking it up over her shoulders before turning her back on him and closing her eyes.

She could still see him, of course, in her mind's eye. His blue eyes so intense he could see into her very soul. She should have recognized him from those eyes. She thought they'd reminded her of Mel Gibson's eyes, but now she knew that the memory was actually her own, from her childhood. Flyboy. Who'd come to her rescue when she felt scared.

Well, she didn't need anyone coming to her rescue anymore. And even if she did, he couldn't save her this time because what she needed rescuing from was her emotions for him. She could still taste him on her lips, lips that were still slightly swollen from the passion of his kisses.

At least she had a partial explanation for why she'd had such an intense reaction to him. They had a past in common and secret feelings of survivor guilt that they shared. Or she'd shared and he'd reluctantly let slip on one occasion.

They'd both grown up in Marine families, both knew the sacrifices and commitment required for that lifestyle.

But she was his commanding officer's daughter, not Princess Pug, not Prudence. And that made her off-limits in his book.

Why did he have to be a Marine? Why couldn't he have joined the Air Force or something?

Maybe that wouldn't have made any difference. Maybe he didn't want a relationship with her in any case. He hadn't said he'd wished things were different.

Maybe he was right and this attraction between them was the result of being snowbound in the mountains with him.

But being marooned with any other Marine wouldn't have affected her the way being stranded with Joe did. It was the man, not the Marine, that got to her as no man ever had before. And that scared her spitless.

Joe didn't even bother trying to get any sleep. He knew it would be utterly useless. His brain was churning with thoughts and his body ached with the need to feel Prudence's soft warmth against him.

He was still grappling with the concept that she was Princess Pug, the kid in pigtails he'd known that summer so long ago. Her hair had been lighter then, streaked by the sun. They'd hung out together, this despite the fact that she was a few years younger than he was. He'd been, what, all of ten at the time.

He was the second youngest of the Wilder brothers—with Mark aka Eagle being the next oldest, and then Justice aka Ranger. Sam aka Champ was the baby in the family, a year younger than Joe. All his brothers were Marines.

While it was true that the Marine Corps was one large family, and that for many the Marine Corps was their family—in his case both were true. Joe had always been able to talk to his brothers if he had any problems. Sure, there was an element of sibling rivalry and competitiveness between them, but there was also a deep bond between them as well.

And yes, it was true that in the past Joe had always made friends easily, but the kind of deep bond he shared with his brothers and with his best friend Curt did not come easily for him.

His thoughts kept wandering as he watched Prudence sleep. He shared a bond with her. One that wasn't just based on sexual chemistry, although there was plenty of that as their kiss and embraces had proved.

She did things to him, made him feel things, made him forget his duty. A Marine prided himself on his control. He almost totally lost it with her.

She wasn't like the other women he'd known. Something was happening between them, something he wasn't sure how to stop. But he had to figure it out ASAP.

He couldn't let her get close to him. Not just because she was his commanding officer's daughter, but because he couldn't let anyone get close to him. Not now. Not when he was so messed up. He knew all about first aid, but he had no idea how to fix this gaping wound inside of him.

And that made him want to lash out, like an injured bear caught in a trap. He didn't want to lash out at Prudence. He didn't want her seeing him for what he really was, a man less than what he'd been—less courageous, less sure of himself, less deserving of being called a United States Marine.

He had to earn those things back, had to recover them somehow.

It was far better to end things before they began.

There was no sense in thinking of how things could have been if he'd been someone else or she'd been someone else. There was no changing the facts. And the facts were that this was a no-win situation.

No amount of maneuvering or strategy would change the bottom line. She was the last woman in the world he could afford to get involved with and he was the worst man in the world for her.

She deserved someone who had their act together, someone who could come to her without the nightmares and baggage he was carrying.

He tensed as she tossed restlessly in her sleeping bag. Silently moving closer, he watched over her, praying her nightmare wouldn't return, wishing he could allow himself the brief luxury of brushing his fingers over her cheek but knowing he had to be strong.

Being strong had never been a problem for him before. Which made his current state so foreign. He wasn't used to feeling helpless. Yet that feeling struck him like an enemy sniper, hitting him when he least expected it.

It wasn't logical. It wasn't acceptable. The Marine Corps values all revolved around honor, courage and commitment.

He had to regain those things or die trying.

Joe's eyes were gritty from three nights of little sleep, but he refused to surrender to exhaustion...and the ensuing nightmares. He'd just close his eyes for a minute, take a ten-minute catnap and wake up refreshed and battle-ready. He'd done it before, he could do that again.

But the dreams came even in that brief period. Or were they hallucinations?

A child by a lake. A scream. Tears. Pulled under by terror until he was drowning in it.

Joe jerked awake. There was an unaccustomed moisture on his face. Lifting trembling fingers, he angrily wiped his cheek.

What the hell was happening to him? Was he losing his mind? He was definitely losing his grip.

Marines must not fail. They also never cried. No matter what.

Prudence stared out the tiny window above the rustic sink and wished she was a million miles away. All morning she'd been sidestepping Joe, trying to ignore his presence. The snow had stopped falling two hours and twenty minutes ago, she knew because she'd checked her watch every ten minutes since she'd awakened shortly after dawn.

Joe was up before the sun. At first she thought he'd left her at the cabin and walked down the mountainside himself, determined to get away from her at all costs. But then he'd come in from outside, his cheeks red from the cold, his arms filled with more firewood.

She'd tried telling herself she wasn't relieved to see him. She'd lied. The sight of him made her knees go weak. He'd looked tired. Tiny lines of exhaustion fanned out from his blue eyes. He'd swapped the khaki-green T-shirt he'd worn under his utility shirt for a gray one.

From that moment until now they'd spoken maybe a dozen words, and most of those had been of the one-syllable variety. "Morning." "Coffee?" "No, thank you."

That was about the extent of their conversation. No reference to the passion they'd shared last night. No mention of the fact that they'd almost made love. No acknowledgment whatsoever that any kind of personal relationship existed between them.

But ignoring it didn't make it go away. She was still as aware of him as she'd ever been. In fact, she was even more aware of him now, because she was trying so hard to ignore him. And because she knew what it was like to have him hold her in his arms and kiss her as if she were the only woman on the planet who could touch his heart.

Prudence checked her watch again. Five more minutes had passed. Weak sunshine was breaking through the departing clouds. Which meant that the rescue helicopter should be coming soon.

She'd tidied the cabin as best she could. The metal tub she'd used for her bath last night was once again resting against the far wall. Her sleeping bag was rolled and tied to her backpack. She'd made a list of the food they'd used and intended to replace it upon her return home so that the next time someone needed to use this cabin in an emergency, they'd have what they needed.

But Prudence didn't have what she needed. She didn't have Joe smiling at her, teasing her, even talking to her. But he was looking at her. Oh, not openly. But even if her back was turned to him, she could tell when his eyes strayed over to her during his brief sojourns into the cabin. Most of the time he spent outside, watching for the helicopter. But when he did come inside, he watched her. Covertly. She could feel his gaze on her. The skin on the back of her neck actually prickled.

She'd gathered her hair into a ponytail and had added a touch of lip gloss in a foolish attempt to keep her spirits up. It hadn't worked.

Joe was watching her now. She could feel his presence a few yards behind her. She turned to confront him, but he was already looking away, intent on making sure the cabin was in order.

"Well, does it pass the inspection?" she said, tired of the silence between them.

"Yes, ma'am."

Her head tilted back as if he'd slapped her. So it was back to *ma'am* now, was it?

Narrowing her eyes at him, she refused to let her emotions show. At least not the sappy emotions. The man had told her himself that it was fine to be aggravated with him. Fine. She was plenty aggravated with him right now.

For the first time since she'd woken that morning his eyes met hers. She didn't look away and neither did he. He had a Marine's talent for disguising his emotions.

Which is why the small flare of passion in his gaze caught her by surprise. Her lips parted and she was about to speak when the sound of an approaching helicopter sliced through the thick silence.

Joe completed a perfect about-face and marched out of the cabin, snagging his pack in one hand and her heavy backpack in the other on the way out.

As Prudence turned to make sure the fire was doused with water, she noted that Joe had tried to pour cold water on the passion they'd shared last night. But unlike the fire, whose embers dutifully died out, the desire she felt for him showed no signs of abating.

Stupid as it sounded, she was actually a bit sad to be leaving the cabin. They'd shared something special here. But it had melted as quickly as the snow beneath the warm spring sunshine outside, leaving a messy quagmire behind. It would be so easy to get bogged down in the mud, to get stuck in the emotional mayhem. But she wouldn't let herself take that path. Stepping outside, she maneuvered around the icy patches, avoided the soggy ground and headed toward the waiting helicopter.

Joe had returned to the cabin to give it a final check. No way would he delegate the responsibility. He'd shoulder it all himself.

The young blond copilot was standing by the helicopter door, flashing her a beachboy's white smile. She welcomed his attention. Here was one man who didn't think of her as Sergeant Major Martin's daughter.

"Sorry for the delay in getting up here." If he called her ma'am, she'd have to hit him, rescue or no rescue. Instead he grinned at her and added, "I hope you won't hold that against me, Prudence."

She smiled and flashed him a flirtatious look. "On the contrary, Bob." She read his name from his flight suit. Unlike the military, here first names were used. "I'm forever in your debt."

"Let me give you a hand there," Bob said, gallantly assisting her into one of the passenger seats of the helicopter.

When Joe hopped aboard a short time later, Prudence was busy silently congratulating herself on how she'd kept her dignity, kept her distance with Joe.

Then she saw his face. It was as gray as the T-shirt he'd been wearing under his utilities. Was he remembering the helicopter that had crashed before his very eyes?

Without thinking, Prudence placed her hand on his arm in a comforting gesture. Big mistake. She should have known better. Joe yanked his arm away from her, his blue eyes fierce in their resolve to keep her away from him.

Prudence had to blink away the tears as she turned to stare blindly out the window. It should not have hurt as much as it did. He'd made it plain last night that he wanted nothing to do with her. Yet still she kept after him. What was wrong with her? Was she that desperate?

Still, how could she turn her back on Flyboy, the young boy who'd helped her in her time of need? How could she deny the bond she'd felt with him from the very beginning?

Maybe in time she'd learn. Right now it was the only hope she could hold on to.

Joe gritted his teeth and hung on to his control. When Prudence had touched him, he'd almost lost it. He'd seen the compassion in her eyes. Was she feeling sorry for him?

He had no doubt he was a sorry sight. A coward

wearing a warrior's uniform. He should never have spilled his guts to her. All she had to do was let her daddy know that Joe was a few pancakes short of a stack and bingo, Joe would be out of the Marines so fast his head would spin. Any whiff of emotional problems or instability would go on his record and hurt his career as a Marine.

Would she do something like that? Earlier this morning she'd looked mad enough to kick his behind herself, without letting her father do it for her.

He clenched his jaw as the possibilities continued to taunt him. She could tell her father so many things—not the least of which was that Joe had made out with her. The fact that he'd befriended her as a kid so long ago wouldn't carry any weight with her father. Joe should have resisted her charms, should have been strong. *Should have, should have, should have.*

He closed his eyes against the all-too-familiar refrain pounding in his head, matching the whirring *whack-whack* of the helicopter's rotor blades as they came in for a landing.

Opening his eyes and looking down, he recognized his commanding officer in the small crowd gathered.

Joe had no memory of actually deplaning. He was running on autopilot, watching as if from afar as Sergeant Major Martin hugged Prudence before turning to face Joe.

Saluting his commanding officer, Joe braced himself, expecting to be held accountable for getting them all snowbound. He'd been responsible for the group. No excuses, no exceptions.

Instead Sergeant Major Martin said, "Good job, Sergeant Wilder."

"Thank you, sir." Joe's voice was military precise, but inside he felt as if a rug had just been yanked out from under him. He'd expected his commanding officer to chew him out and then forbid him from ever seeing his precious daughter again.

But in the end it was Joe who forbade himself from seeing Prudence as he walked away from her without a backward glance.

"Your mother was worried about you, but I told her that Sergeant Wilder would take good care of you," her father said as he pulled up in front of Prudence's rental house. "She's cooking up a storm inside. Made your favorite meal. Beef Stroganoff with all the trimmings. We figured you'd insist on coming here instead of going home with us tonight."

"This *is* my home," Prudence said as she got out of her father's sport utility vehicle. The house was a small frame cookie-cutter design that would have looked like its anonymous neighbors were it not for the special touches Prudence had added—the colorful butterfly wind sock, the cheerful terra cotta pots brimming with red geraniums, the wicker rocking chair she'd found at a local flea market and repainted herself.

The minute Prudence saw her mom puttering in the kitchen, she felt tears come to her eyes. Ellen Martin hadn't changed her pert short haircut in the past decade. A bit shorter than Prudence, she shared her daughter's brown eyes and giving nature. The older woman just looked so heartwarming, so real and so like...*mom*. And despite the fact that Prudence was a full-grown woman, in that moment her mom represented everything that was true and safe in the world.

Having just talked about the car accident with Joe had brought all those memories tumbling back—the blind fear, the guilt, the relief, the undying gratitude.

Prudence heard Joe's voice in her head. *Your situation isn't the same. You mother didn't die. She recovered.*

A minute later Prudence was in her mom's arms.

"Ah, well." Her father cleared his throat as he hastily backed out of the kitchen. "I'll just leave you two girls alone and wrap some things up back at the base. I'll be back in half an hour," he said, showing a typical Marine's aversion to tears and emotional scenes as he made his escape.

"I didn't go to the airport to meet you because I knew I'd turn into a watering can and get all weepy," her mom, Ellen, told her with a rueful laugh and a swipe at her damp cheeks.

"I would have started crying, too," Prudence agreed, stepping back to wipe her own cheeks with a paper towel she grabbed from the hanger near the sink.

"I could have told your father I was just cutting onions for the Stroganoff and that's why I had tears in my eyes, but that would have been a lie. I'm just so glad to see you!" Ellen grabbed Prudence and hugged her again.

"I'm glad to see you, too, Mom." Prudence fiercely returned the hug. "Real glad."

"So tell me everything that happened," Ellen said, tugging a white bar stool closer so that Prudence could sit beside her as she sat on another stool and chopped fresh mushrooms.

Looking around the kitchen, Prudence felt a sense of unreality.

Only an hour earlier, she'd still been snowbound

with Joe. Yet here she was, surrounded by familiar things—the red rooster canister set, the fresh chives growing on her windowsill, the black-and-white ceramic tiles that were original to the house when it was first built back in the 1950s. When she'd first moved into the house those tiles had driven her crazy. Just like when she'd first met Joe he'd driven her crazy. Then she'd grown to love the tiles for their uniqueness, just as she'd grown to love Joe.

Panic hit her. She loved Joe? Where had that come from? Looking around her kitchen wasn't supposed to bring a moment of epiphany like that. No, momentous discoveries like that didn't happen during nondescript moments like this. Looking at her kitchen tiles wouldn't make her realize she loved Joe.

Her knees were shaky as she sank onto the bar stool. Shoot. She loved Joe. She was definitely in deep trouble here.

Now what was she supposed to do? The man had walked away from her without a backward glance.

Unrequited love really stinks, she decided morosely, reaching for a cookie stashed in the largest of the rooster canisters.

"Prudence?" her mom asked, a frown of concern on her forehead.

"Do you remember that summer when we were in Okinawa when I was a kid?" Prudence said as she munched on her Oreo.

Ellen blinked at the non sequitur before nodding. "Sure, I remember. You were not a happy camper at the time."

"I don't know if I mentioned it then, but there was a kid that made the summer bearable for me. That kid was Sergeant Joe Wilder."

"Is that why your dad arranged for him to accompany you up into the mountains?"

Prudence was surprised by her mother's question. "No. Sergeant Brown was supposed to come with us but he had to have emergency surgery so Joe was called in to take his place."

"He was?" Ellen blinked and then frowned. "I had no idea. I wish your father had told me that Sergeant Brown was in the hospital. I would have gone to visit him." She dumped the chopped mushrooms into a hot skillet. "I'll have to drop by sick bay tomorrow and see how he's doing. But getting back to you and this Joe, did you recognize him right away?"

"No. And he didn't recognize me, either. In fact, when we first met at the base he thought that I was a sixth-grader. I mean, he'd been told to give his commanding officer's daughter's sixth-grade class a tour of the base so he naturally thought that I was..."

"That you were what?" Ellen promoted.

"One of the students." Prudence replied.

"The scuttlebutt around the base is that he's something of a ladies' man and that he's into some pretty risky things like bungee-jumping," Ellen noted with concern as she checked on the noodles before turning down the heat a bit. "Your father wasn't pleased about that. But he didn't seemed concerned that this Joe would take risks with you or the kids, so maybe the gossip isn't true."

"What gossip?"

Ellen wiped her hands on a kitchen towel before replying. "That Wilder isn't just his name, it's his lifestyle. He doesn't appear to have done anything inappropriate with you, though."

Prudence wondered how inappropriate her mother

would think it was to have almost made love with Joe last night. To Prudence it had seemed the most appropriate thing in the world at the time. Because she was in love with Joe.

The question was, what was she going to do about it?

Over the next few days Joe made the unwelcome discovery that out of sight did not mean out of mind where Prudence was concerned. Everything reminded him of her. He'd see the night sky and remember her perched on that boulder, her head turned as she looked at him. He'd drink a cold beer and remember how he'd likened her appeal to that of a cold beer after a long march when he'd first met her.

The thing was, he hadn't just met her a few days ago. They'd really first met when they'd been kids, when she'd been Princess Pug and he'd been Flyboy.

Over the years Joe had come to believe that Fate did work in mysterious ways. But that didn't stop him from trying to understand it. Why had Prudence reappeared in his life now, after all this time? Why couldn't he believe her when she said he wasn't to blame for the accident? How could he know that in his mind yet not accept it in his heart?

He went about his duties like a good Marine. He was temporarily stationed at Camp Lejeune until his orders came through for his next tour of duty. He was up for a promotion and there had been talk of sending him on a recruiting rotation. The Corps sent its best to bring in the next generation of Marines.

It wasn't an assignment Joe was looking forward to. But then it was almost impossible to advance within the Corps without doing a tour of duty as a recruiting officer. So he'd do his duty. And then he'd move on, as he always did.

Just as he'd done his duty by accompanying Prudence and the kids...very short recruits...on that trip into the mountains.

His commanding officer had made no mention of the fact that Joe had kissed Prudence, nor had he commented on Joe's possible instability—which had to mean that Prudence hadn't said anything to her father about either potentially explosive situation.

Which wasn't to say that she wouldn't blab something at some point in the future. A part of his heart told him that she wasn't the type to betray a confidence, but another part of him berated his own stupidity in allowing himself to become this vulnerable.

Joe welcomed his weekend liberty and the chance to get off the base. He was living in the barracks, but it was nice to get away for a while—away from the memory of Prudence and the heat of her kisses.

The nightmares had returned every night, repeating the disturbing dream he'd had in the cabin that last night. Water. A child. Screams. Terror. The suffocating feeling of drowning.

He told himself it must be an aftereffect of being responsible for the very short recruits last weekend. Well, this weekend was going to be different.

One of his bungee-jumping buddies had given him a call, asking for his help with a group doing a jump Saturday morning. Joe wouldn't be jumping himself so he wouldn't be disobeying orders by helping out.

While driving out to the site in his Jeep, Joe reminded himself that he'd done the right thing walking away from Prudence. Being with her would lead to nothing but trouble.

Ah, but what sweet trouble. The chemistry between them was an incredible thing. He had enough experience with women to know that what they'd shared didn't come around the block every day. In fact, he'd never experienced the instant explosion of desire he'd felt with Prudence.

The jump site was a man-made tower built near the ocean, near enough to tourists and thrill-seekers visiting the coastal cities like Wilmington.

His buddy Beau, who'd made a killing in the dot-com marketplace, had moved on to a new dream of starting up an adventure tour company featuring local North Carolina sites—whitewater rafting, hang-gliding or bungee-jumping. The bungee tower had been a huge hit.

There was a small crowd gathered around the tower by the time Joe got there.

Since the haunting dreams had kept Joe awake most of the night, he had a desperate need for caffeine to jump-start his nervous system. The large paper cup of black coffee in his hand should be just the ticket. He was just about to take a large sip when he saw her.

Stunned, Joe almost spilled the hot coffee down the front of his T-shirt.

Maybe he was seeing things?

He blinked, but she was still there when he opened his eyes.

Swearing under his breath, he marched up to Prudence and confronted her. "What are you doing here?" he demanded.

Her warm smile aroused his body but her words... her words chilled him to the bone. "I'm getting ready to go bungee-jumping."

Chapter Nine

"Are you out of your mind?" Joe growled.

"You bungee-jump," Prudence retorted. "Are *you* out of *your* mind?"

He glared at her. "What is this? Some kind of test to prove I'm reckless, that I'm a pancake or two short of a stack? You think showing up like this is going to make me admit anything?"

She frowned at him. "Admit what?"

So many things. That he wanted her with every breath he took. That he was tired of the nightmares consuming him. That he was losing faith that he'd ever be the man he used to be.

Prudence watched the conflicted emotions flashing over Joe's face and desperately wished she could decipher them. She'd spent the first twenty-four hours apart from Joe moping, returning to school and her class with outward calm while inside she felt such a huge, gaping sense of loss.

What they'd shared was special—the kisses, the embraces, the gleam in his eyes when he'd teased her and the shadows of darkness when he'd confessed his secret feelings of guilt to her. He'd told her things she was sure he hadn't said to anyone else. And they were things he needed to say.

Joe Wilder needed *her*. Whether he knew it or not. And she needed him. If she wanted him—and she did—then she was going to do something about it.

She wasn't going to let him walk away without putting up a fight. She'd spent the past ten years being so cautious, so afraid of making another mistake that she'd just about stopped living. It was time to start taking risks again. Her feelings for Joe had taught her that much.

There was a time for caution and a time for taking a leap of faith—in this case a literal leap.

So she'd signed up for bungee-jumping from one of Joe's buddies. It hadn't taken much questioning around the base to find out who his bungee-jumping friends were. And when she discovered that one of them was offering a bungee-jumping experience this weekend, she'd signed up.

She hadn't known Joe would show up, although she'd certainly anticipated that possibility. And having anticipated that, you'd think she'd have come up with something brilliant to say to him. She hadn't. Not yet.

Maybe after she'd bungee-jumped she'd find the words. She'd heard that the experience was great for your self-esteem, that you experienced a huge sense of achievement.

Maybe she'd end up being transformed into a self-confident drop-dead gorgeous femme fatale.

Wait, maybe drop dead wasn't the best description to use—given the fact that she was jumping off a seventy-foot-high tower. And maybe *fatale* wasn't all that good, either, she decided with a nervous swallow.

"I forbid you to go bungee-jumping," Joe declared.

She blinked at him. "You're kidding, right?"

"Your father…"

"Isn't your concern," she firmly stated, narrowing her eyes at him in a warning he ignored.

He stopped her departure with a hand on her arm. "He's my commanding officer."

"And you're afraid he'll blame you for making me go bungee-jumping? Well, I'm not living my life in fear any longer." She yanked her arm away from his hold.

"You clearly haven't thought this through."

"A good plan violently executed now is better than a perfect plan executed next week."

Joe recognized the quote. "You're no General Patton," he told her.

She merely lifted her chin at him and fixed him with a schoolteacher's stare. The kind that got you sent to the principal's office.

But Joe was long past being impressed by schoolyard techniques. "You came here today to get revenge on me for kissing you up at the cabin."

Her mouth dropped open. "Excuse me?"

"You heard me. You're furious that I walked away from you, so you came up with this ridiculous idea to try to get my attention."

Well, he was partially right. She had wanted to get his attention. But the bungee-jump had taken on a meaning of its own for her now. It represented a way out of the fear and caution she'd cocooned herself in and it had become a hurdle she had to overcome in order for the old Prudence to reemerge.

"You probably had no intention of ever jumping, you just showed up here to get under my skin," he said.

"First off, I had no way of knowing you'd be here. Secondly, I have every intention of jumping. Just watch me, Flyboy."

"Go home," Joe said flatly. "You don't belong here." He turned and walked away from her yet again.

Joe found his buddy Beau ready to head up with the first group of jumpers. "Hey, buddy, I need you to check the weigh-ins," Beau told Joe. Getting an accurate weight on each individual was important because the number of rubber cords used was determined by the jumper's weight and people had a tendency to lie about something like that.

Joe was distracted by a blond beach bunny in a halter top asking him a question. The next time he looked up, Beau had taken his group to the top of the tower.

"They're not going to toss you off the tower, you'll be jumping. That's why it's called bungee-jumping and not bungee-tossing," Joe told the blonde, sending her one of his patented grins.

But he felt no pleasure in the curvy blonde's interest. He was still rattled by seeing Prudence. Thank heaven he'd seen Prudence heading back to her car after he'd read her the riot act.

"Hey, Joe, your friend is about to take her jump," Beau's younger brother Brady said.

"What friend?" Joe asked, sudden dread filling his stomach.

"The cute schoolteacher. Patience...no Prudence. That's her name."

"Oh God." He looked up.

Joe thought he knew fear. But until he saw Prudence hanging in midair he realized he knew nothing, except that this woman got to him as no other ever had.

Joe was waiting for her when Prudence came down from the tower. The minute her feet were on terra firma he grabbed her by the arm and hustled her off to a stand of palmetto palms away from the rest of the crowd.

"I told you to go home," he growled.

"And I told you that I was going bungee-jumping." Her cheeks were flushed, her eyes wide with wonder. "Wow. That was incredible!"

"I'll tell you what that was." Each word was gritted out between clenched teeth. "That was the first and last time you are ever doing anything that reckless."

"It wasn't reckless," she argued, still caught up in the adrenaline of the experience. "I just sort of leaned forward and by the time I started having second thoughts I was already doing it."

"Well you're never doing it again."

"Why not? It's relatively safe. Your friend told me that his safety record is perfect. He told me about the history of bungee-jumping, starting with the tribespeople of the Pentecost Islands over a thousand years ago. Did you know that legend has it that the first bungee-jumper was a woman trying to escape her cruel husband? She climbed a banyan tree and, when he followed her, she tied some liana vines around her ankles and jumped. He leaped after her and ended up plunging to his death, but the vines saved her from crashing into the ground. They had enough give that she bounced back."

Joe didn't know if he'd ever bounce back from the scare she'd given him.

"Bungee-jumping may seem like a death-defying act, but the flexible cord cushions the fall," Prudence was saying. "I researched it on the Internet. Parachutists and pole vaulters actually experience a harder jolt."

"So, what, you're going to take up pole vaulting and parachuting next? You are crazy!"

The more agitated he got, the calmer she got. "Explain to me again why you can go bungee-jumping, off a bridge, not a controlled situation like this one, and it's fine."

"Because I've had more experience than you have."

"I'm trying to get more experience," she said.

"Not on my watch."

"You're not on duty here, Sergeant. You've got no authority over my actions. You better than anyone should know how many safety precautions they take here. The cords are inspected before each jump, ditto for all the equipment and harnesses. Beau said the cords are retired after three hundred jumps, sometimes even earlier."

Hearing her recite statistics Joe had often told others was like being tossed into in the Twilight Zone. Nothing she was saying was making him feel any better. He was still furious...and badly shaken.

"This is my fault!" he shouted because talking to her in a reasonable tone didn't seem to be working. "You told me yourself that you were a cautious person. Then I got you snowbound—"

"The blizzard got us snowbound," she interrupted to correct him but he ignored her words.

"—and the stress was too much. I drove you over the edge. Made you revert to your former reckless behavior."

Cupping his cheek with one hand, she guided his face to hers, using her free hand to point to her own eyes. "Look at me when you're yelling at me, Sergeant." She waited until his startled blue eyes met hers. "And listen to what I have to say. Since you won't say a word in your own defense, I'll do it for you." Her touch softened as she smoothed her hand down his cheek in a move that was both a caress and a benediction. "You're not to blame for the helicopter crash, or for getting us snowbound, or for me choosing to go bungee-jumping. You are not responsible. It's not your fault. I've actually wanted to go bungee-jumping since I was a teenager, but I told myself I shouldn't do it after the car accident. And that was wrong. I was living in fear. Fear of being myself. I don't want to live that way anymore."

"So that means what?" His eyes burned into hers.

"I don't know what it means," she answered honestly. "But I can tell you this much. I know you're not ready to deal with your survivor guilt yet and I can understand that. Believe me, I've been there. But I'm not giving up on you, even if you've given up on yourself."

He looked away. "If you know as much about survival guilt as you say you do, then you know that logical statements don't have any effect on the guilt."

"I just want you to know that you're not alone anymore," she said.

"I've never been alone," he shot back, stepping away from her.

She smiled as if she knew his thoughts. "We've

both been alone, in one way or another. You may not have been alone in the past, but you've been alone lately. Very alone. That doesn't have to be the case anymore. I'm not giving up on you.''

"You should," he muttered.

"Let me be the judge of that. So are you hungry?'' she cheerfully inquired.

He blinked at her. "Hungry?"

"That's right. Hungry. As for food.''

As opposed to what? Being hungry for her kisses?

"When was the last time you ate?'' she asked him.

"What are you, my mother?'' Joe replied irritably.

"After that jump, I just have this tremendous awareness of everything—the sunlight, the smell of the ocean, the image of fried clams from Sonny's. Have you had their fried clams since you got here? No? Then you haven't tasted heaven.''

He didn't know about that. Kissing her had sure tasted like heaven to him.

"Come on," she coaxed him. "My treat. The best fried clams in the world are only a few minutes' drive from here. What do you say?''

He should say no way, if he had any sense at all. But for some reason he said yes. Maybe it was the look in her eyes, so filled with anticipation and laughter. Or maybe it was the prospect of spending time with her after facing the raw fear of losing her.

He should still be furious with her, and part of him was. But Joe had never been one to hold a grudge, and for some reason he didn't seem able to resist her right now. His defenses were definitely at a disadvantage at the moment. It was as if she were a stealth bomber who'd slipped beneath his radar detection and scored a direct hit on his heart.

She was in the passenger seat of his Jeep, her small backpack/purse in hand, before he knew what happened. "Put your seat belt on," he growled at her.

She wrinkled her nose at his tone of voice but obeyed his order. "Nice Jeep," she noted as he backed out of the lot and down the small road that lead to the main highway.

He wasn't going to let her charm him that easily. "Where's this Sonny's place located?"

"Two miles north of here. They're located right off the highway." Undoing her ponytail, she shook her head and let her hair fall around her shoulders in what Joe considered to be an altogether too sexy manner. Next she removed her cardigan, revealing the pink T-shirt she wore beneath it. The stretchy material molded to her breasts like a lover's hand, the way his hand had cupped her sweetness.

His palms itched with the need to cup her lush breasts once again, to hold them and caress them with a brush of his fingertips, making her moan in pleasure as she had in the cabin.

"The speed limit along here is thirty-five not fifty-five," she noted with a glance at the Jeep's speedometer.

Silently swearing, he let up on the gas pedal.

She said, "So you're a leadfoot huh?"

A portion of his body was definitely as hard as lead, but it wasn't his foot. Joe shifted in the driver's seat, the fit of his jeans tight and uncomfortable. Her hand on his thigh only made matters worse.

"You just passed Sonny's," she told him, nodding with her head toward the restaurant he could see in the rearview mirror.

Agreeing to eat with her was a big mistake. He

could see that now. He should just take her back to her own car and dump her there. Before he did something he'd regret.

As if aware that she might have pushed him too far, Prudence removed her hand and stopped giving him those heated sideways looks that raised his blood pressure into the danger zone.

Instead she efficiently directed him to a place where he could turn around. They reached Sonny's two minutes later and Joe jumped out of the Jeep as if he'd been strapped to an ejection seat. He opened the passenger door for her, his training as a Marine requiring the courtesy. Smiling, she nodded her thanks.

Sonny's was not the place for a romantic rendezvous. The place was well-lit and busy, with all the red-checkered plastic tableclothed tables filled to capacity. Faith Hill was crooning from a pair of speakers while the sound of the ocean drifted in through the screened porch area.

Joe relaxed. The smell of food made his mouth water. So did the sight of her, a few minutes later, daintily dipping clams into red sauce before popping them into her mouth.

She even closed her eyes and murmured *mmm* in the ultimate sign of satisfaction. Did she look that way when she made love? If he hadn't pulled away from her, if they had made love that night in the cabin, would she have looked up at him and murmured *mmm* when he gave her the ultimate satisfaction?

"You're not eating," she noted as she opened her eyes and gazed at him in concern. "Don't you like it?"

"Are you deliberately trying to drive me crazy?" he growled.

"By eating fried clams in front of you?" She grinned at him, a dab of red seafood sauce on her upper lip. Joe wanted to kiss it from her mouth.

Grabbing a paper napkin from the metal holder on the table, he shoved it at her. "You've got sauce on your mouth."

Instead of taking the napkin, she sent her tongue in search of the errant sauce.

Oh Lord. He was dying here.

She was doing it deliberately, he was sure of it. Well, heck, two could play at that game. Male/female games were right up his alley.

"Here." Reaching out, he gently brushed his index finger over her upper lip. "There, that's better." Bringing his finger to his own mouth, he sucked the sauce that had been on her lips into his own mouth. "Mmm, that is good."

She was staring at him with eyes that were cloudy with desire. She should have known he'd be better at this flirting stuff than she was. But she hadn't been able to resist teasing him just a little.

Now she was having second thoughts. It never paid to tweak a tiger's tail. It was bound to turn around and take a huge bite out of you if you weren't careful.

Of course, she'd vowed to stop being so careful, and frankly the idea of him taking a bite out of her— huge or otherwise—was infinitely appealing and downright sexy. The man gave her hot flashes.

He looked awesome in jeans and a black T-shirt. It was the first time she'd seen him in civilian clothes and she had to admit she wanted to see more of him. She remembered every ripple of muscle beneath that T-shirt.

With his close-cropped dark hair and vivid blue

eyes, he was garnering plenty of attention from the female diners. *Hands off, girls,* she wanted to say. *He's mine.*

When he caught her staring at him, she had to say something. "So who broke your nose?"

Oh great, that was real smooth, she thought to herself in disgust.

He laughed. She loved the sound of his laughter. It was rich and addictive, like coffee ice cream.

"I did," he admitted. "A few months after leaving Okinawa. We were stationed in Oklahoma and I was an altar boy. Only a clumsy one as it turns out. My brothers called me falter boy. I tripped over the hem of my altar boy robe and fell flat on my face."

"So instead of Flyboy maybe I should call you Falter Boy, huh?"

"Only my brothers can get away with that."

She ate a forkful of creamy coleslaw before commenting. "You know, I envy you having siblings. It must have made the moving around a little easier, because they came with you and you weren't alone. As I recall, you're all only a few years apart in age."

"That's right. There's only a year or two between one brother and the next."

"That must have been nice."

He shrugged. While he loved his brothers, talking about them made him uneasy for some reason. Maybe it was just his overall condition of being messed up, he noted darkly.

"The moving around can be hard," she admitted. "But my parents did everything they could to make it an adventure. We'd call it establishing base camp and while we didn't have much furniture, we always used the same living-room drapes to make wherever we were seem like home. And I always had my books. I brought them with me, and those characters in my favorite stories became friends that traveled with me."

"You made friends along the way. What about that princess you were telling me about?"

"Vanessa? Yes, we did become friends." Prudence nibbled on another fried clam. "I think partially because we had that in common, the fact that we both had led unusual lives compared to the other girls at the ritzy school."

"A Marine brat like you at a ritzy school?"

She laughed. "Yeah, I know. I told my dad it was a bad idea. I got tossed out after two years. For organizing a student strike on behalf of the cafeteria workers. But Vanessa and I have kept in touch over the years." Daintily dabbing her lips with a napkin, she paused to look at him. "Do we have time for dessert?"

"Depends what it is." If she was the dessert, he'd make time.

"Lemon sherbet. The best in the state. They make it right here. Are you game?"

Game? He was primed and ready. But not for sherbet. For *her.*

"I think I've had enough." Even his voice sounded tight.

"Do you mind if I get some sherbet?" She gave him a guileless look before adding, "You can taste some of mine if you want."

Oh, he *wanted* all right. Wanted her so much he ached. Watching her as she sensually licked the sherbet from her spoon a few minutes later only made things worse.

"Want some?" she asked with a saucy smile.

Instead of replying, Joe simply leaned forward and kissed her, bracing his hand against the back of her head as he hungrily licked the icy sherbet from her warm lips.

He broke off the kiss before she could do more than gasp—with pleasure or outrage. He couldn't be sure until he sat back. Then the bemused softness in her brown eyes told him that he'd gotten to her.

"Very tasty," he noted huskily.

"Mmm," she murmured. "Very tasty. Want more?"

"I can't," he said regretfully.

"I know." She sighed. "This isn't the time nor place."

"I'd better drive you back to your car." Because the more time he spent with her, the more he wanted to make love with her.

The short ride back was accompanied by the sound of the Jeep's radio. The Eurythmics "Sweet Dreams" was playing on the local light rock station.

As Joe approached her car, she said, "Did Principal Vann get in touch with you yet? He said he was going to call you about coming to speak at the school. Keishon, Gem, Pete, Rosa and Sinatra have been raving about you, and the other kids in the other classes would like to meet you."

"I can picture Sinatra raving, but I can't see Keishon speaking that highly of me. After all, I chopped down evergreen branches."

"She's forgiven you for that," Prudence noted with a grin.

"She still wearing those T-shirts?"

Prudence nodded. "She wore her Mean and Green one again the other day."

Joe smiled.

"So are you willing to come to the school?" When he paused, she added, "If you'd rather not do that, I understand."

The sympathy in her voice was like a bullet to his pride. "I'll be there first thing Monday morning."

"You don't have to prove anything..."

"I said I'd be there," he stated curtly.

"Okay. I'll see you then." Kissing his cheek, she hopped out of the car, leaving him before he could leave her.

Which made Joe discover something—that he really didn't like being the one she left behind.

Chapter Ten

"So, buddy, how was your wilderness weekend?"

"Who is this?" Joe demanded into his cell phone.

"Nice avoidance technique, but you called me, remember?" Curt said.

"Yeah, I remember," Joe said irritably, staring at the distant horizon. Sunlight beat down on his head and the warm humid air washed over him, filled with the smell of the ocean. He wasn't exactly sure why he'd been drawn to the beach...something to do with the water. The image of water and drowning had crept into his nightmares and now here he was, sitting on a stupid sandy beach like some kind of lost kid. "Have I ever seemed strange to you?"

"All the time," Curt instantly replied with a dry humor he'd never possessed before becoming a father. "So what else is new?"

"The fact that I can't get rid of these damn nightmares."

"Is it the helo crash?" Curt asked, his voice dead serious now.

"It was. In the beginning. But now I'm getting this weird nightmare about drowning. And there's a kid there. A real little kid. Younger than Blue even."

"Have you talked to anyone?" Curt asked.

"I'm talking to you," Joe irritably replied.

"Where are you?"

"I'm on weekend liberty."

"Where?"

"On some deserted beach watching the ocean." Joe filtered a handful of tiny seashells through his fingers. The sand here was gritty and rough—not conducive to welcoming sunbathers and swimmers. Which was a good thing. He didn't want to be around a lot of other people right now.

"I mean where exactly are you? You're still in North Carolina, right?"

"Affirmative. What, did you think I was going to go UA?" The acronym stood for Unauthorized Absence. In his dad's day, it was known as going AWOL.

"Negative," Curt replied. "I just wanted to place you, that's all. And I wanted to identify that strange noise in the background."

"It's the ocean." He paused a minute to stare down at his bare feet, clenched in the sand as he sat on the beach and stared at waves coming in. "You remember boot camp?"

"Sure I do. It's where we met."

"It's where we became Marines," Joe added.

"You were *always* a Marine," Curt said.

That's what Joe used to think. Now he wasn't so sure. About anything.

"Talk to me, buddy. What's going on. You want me to come down there?" Curt asked gruffly.

"And have your wife shoot me? I don't think so."

"She'd understand."

"Maybe, but I don't understand." Joe tossed a broken shell aside. "I did something really stupid."

"Stupider than putting Heat in my jock strap?" Curt inquired with a teasing laugh.

Using humor as a shield was a well-honored tradition in the Marine Corps, and Joe recognized it as such. "Yeah, stupider than that."

"This I've gotta hear."

"I kissed my commanding officer's daughter," Joe admitted. "We were snowbound together in this cabin…"

"Whoa, slow down a minute there," Curt interrupted him to order. "I thought the schoolteacher had a bunch of her students with her."

"She did. And we all got snowbound by this unexpected snowstorm. Something like twenty-four inches fell in twenty-four hours. It was that thick, heavy kind of snow that accumulates quickly. Anyway, I got the VCRs—"

"VCRs?" Curt interrupted him again to ask.

"Vertically Challenged Recruits. That's how I thought of her students. Not as kids, but as very short recruits, or vertically challenged recruits, or even as preadolescents. Made me feel better about the situation."

"Hey, whatever works."

"So I got the VCRs and Prudence, that's the Sergeant Major's daughter, I got us all to a rangers' cabin. They took the kids out by helo the next day, but Prudence and I were left behind for the next trip. Only the storm moved in again and our rescue was delayed for another twenty-six hours."

"So you were counting the hours, huh?"

"Yeah." Joe shifted his brooding gaze from the horizon to the shore, where sunlight reflected off the incoming waves. "We got…close."

"You had sex with your commanding officer's daughter?"

"No, I did not have sex with her. But I wanted to."

"And what did she want?"

"The same thing."

"Oh, man."

"Yeah," Joe agreed glumly. "Oh, man, is right."

"Does the Sergeant Major know?"

"I don't think so," Joe replied.

"Are you afraid she's going to say something to him?"

"I don't think she will. I saw her today. She scared ten years off my life by going bungee-jumping, even though I told her not to."

"Sounds like quite a lady. I can't wait to meet her."

"You don't understand. Nothing can come of this," Joe insisted, knocking over the pile of seashells he'd accumulated. "I'm dealing with stuff and I'm not fit for much of anything right now."

"The nightmares," Curt noted quietly.

"Yeah, the nightmares. And the regrets. The guilt."

"I hear you. No excuses no exceptions. That's the Marine way. But it sucks sometimes."

"Yeah, it does." Joe frowned at a seagull that got too close. It quickly hopped away before swooping back up into the sky.

"You know," Curt said, "Jessie told me something that I've never forgotten. It hit me damn hard, especially that time when Blue went missing from her pre-school. I was explaining to Jessie that warriors never cry and she said that sometimes warriors make others cry.''

''You're saying I'm going to make Prudence cry?'' Joe said. ''Believe me, I've already thought of that, even though she was raised in the Corps and should be used to warriors by now.''

''No, that's not what I meant,'' Curt denied. ''I'm saying that sometimes we get so focused on battening down our own emotional hatches that we lock out the people who care about us the most. You know I ba-sically tried to raise Blue by the Marine Corps Pro-cedure Manual. The Corps taught us some damn good values, like respect and honor, commitment and loy-alty. And those are all great things, valuable things. But so is love.''

''I never said I love Prudence.'' In his book, not saying it meant it wasn't so. He'd put a lot of energy into building an emotional wall around himself since the accident, and he wasn't going to let one incredibly stubborn and incredibly sexy woman smash it down. She'd already gotten too close to him, and he couldn't love her.

Curt's tone was wryly sympathetic as he said, ''Hey, when I was courting Jessie and asked for your advice, I never said I loved her, either. As I recall, you told me that romance is a battlefield filled with land mines, so you've got to tread carefully or get blown to bits. That was your Wilderism for the day.''

''Yeah, well, I seem to have run out of Wilder-isms,'' Joe confessed in a low voice. ''Did I tell you that I actually met Prudence when we were kids? We didn't realize it until we were alone in the cabin and she talked about her past. We spent part of one summer together. Small world, huh?''

''The Marine Corps is one big family.''

''That may be, but I don't think the Sergeant Major would be very pleased at having me join his family. You know how the Marine Corps is about the subject of dating within the Corps. That's allowed in the Navy and Army, within certain guidelines. But it's not allowed in the Marine Corps. And like I said, I've got to get my head straight first, before I do anything else.''

''I'm here for you, buddy.'' Curt's steady voice resonated with rock-solid conviction. ''Whenever you want to talk. Night or day.''

''Thanks. I appreciate that.'' But after Joe ended the call, he couldn't help wondering if the nightmares were permanent. Maybe there was no cure. Maybe this was as good as it got. Or maybe it just got worse.

It had been years since Joe had stepped foot in a middle school principal's office. Despite that fact, not much seemed to have changed. Oh sure, there were more computers, but the place still smelled the same—a unique combination of old gym shoes and badly cooked cafeteria food. Lasagna must be on the menu today.

Actually the smell reminded him of ''Mess and Maintenance Week'' during book camp when he and Curt had been assigned to mess duty, working fifteen hours in the mess hall—washing pots, scrubbing trays. Real glamorous work. But it taught him team work, because if the guys didn't work together, the work didn't get done.

He was on his own here, though. No fellow Marines to back him up.

A young woman behind the high counter gave him an appreciative smile before moving forward. Joe was wearing his dress blues today. Best uniform of any branch of the Armed Forces, with its high-necked navy-blue jacket with red piping and brass buttons and sky-blue trousers. White gloves. White cover—or hat in civilian terminology.

The uniform never failed to get to the ladies. Not that that's why he wore it. He wasn't trying to impress any female, certainly not Prudence. He was here representing his beloved U.S. Marine Corps and therefore he needed to put his best foot forward. Hence the dress blues.

"May I help you?" the young woman inquired with a Southern drawl native to most North Carolinians.

Prudence hadn't picked up a drawl like that yet. And still she was sexy, even with a schoolteacher's voice.

"Sergeant Wilder here to see Principal Vann, ma'am," Joe stated.

"I'll take him," Prudence said from behind him.

He pivoted to find her standing in the doorway from the hallway. Her cheeks were flushed and her breathing was fast as if she'd just been running. He felt the same way himself.

She looked great. Since when had teachers looked this good? She was wearing a skirt. He'd never seen her in a skirt before. It was black and it ended far too high above her knees. What was she doing, showing off that much leg? Air whooshed out of his lungs and blood rushed to forbidden body parts.

A second look told him that her skirt wasn't a macromini, after all. It was actually longer than the skirt of the young assistant behind the counter. It just packed a powerful punch, that's all. She really did have awesome legs. Even her sandals were sexy.

And then there was that top Prudence was wearing. It was the pink of the inside of a seashell and it clung to her body, outlining her breasts. Surely in his day his middle school teacher hadn't had breasts. How was a kid expected to get any work done with a Victoria's Secret seductress like her around? How was a Marine expected not to drool?

The principal's office was air-conditioned, but Joe felt hot. Very hot.

"I'll take him," Prudence repeated.

And I'll take you. The thought shot through his brain like a rocket. He wanted to just toss her over his shoulder and head out, like a conquering hero.

"Ah, there are you, Sergeant." A man's voice distracted Joe from his fantasies. "I'm Principal Vann." The man stepping out from an office in the back was in his late forties, the same age as Prudence's father and Joe's commanding officer. But where the Sergeant Major had the physically fit body of a warrior, Principal Vann had the body of a civilian, though he had a firm handshake. Principal Vann's eyes reflected intelligence and his smile reflected the people skills of a good politician. "We're so glad you were able to come visit our school today. We've got the entire school gathered in the gymnasium for a special assembly." Principal Vann checked the time on the large clock on the wall. Another thing that hadn't changed—those black clocks with white faces. "We'd better get along down there or we'll be late. I certainly wouldn't want to be accused to detaining a U.S. Marine. After you, Sergeant.'' The principal ushered him through the door leading back out to the hallway.

As Joe took that long walk down the hallway, he was reminded of the long walk he'd taken back at the base to the conference room where Prudence had been waiting for him. She walked beside him now.

He kept his gaze straight ahead, refusing to allow himself to be distracted by the hauntingly familiar scent of her perfume. Where was this damn gymnasium, in Georgia?

Finally they reached their destination. The place was decorated up the wazoo with streamers and bunting. A long banner was painted in red, white and blue—Dixon Middle School Welcomes... *Sargent* was crossed out and replaced with Sergeant Wilder.

Marines Rock! proclaimed another sign.

The chorus and band was gathered on a special stand of bleachers with their music director standing before them, hands raised, sheet music ready as they burst into a loud rendition of The Marines' Hymn.

Standing at attention and staring out at the crowd of kids, Joe felt raw panic blasting away at his insides.

He could handle this. He *would* handle this. A Marine must not fail.

After the song, Principal Vann stepped forward to address the students. ''We're very proud to have a special guest with us this morning. Sergeant Joe Wilder is the U.S. Marine who helped to save five of our students when that unexpected spring snowstorm stranded them all in the mountains. I've asked him to come today to talk to you about that experience.''

As Joe walked across the gymnasium floor to the podium, he noticed a group of boys shooting spitballs as each other in the last row. Had he ever been that young?

A wooden podium had been set up for him directly beneath the basketball basket. Red, white and blue bunting was draped across the front of it and the American flag was on display beside him.

Stepping up to the microphone he began speaking.

Joe had no idea what he said. He had no idea if any of it made any sense. He kept his eyes straight ahead, his gaze fixed on the scoreboard located at the other end of the gym.

Sweat gathered above his upper lip and his ears began to roar. Yet still he continued speaking, his curt voice possessing the barklike tenor of a drill sergeant presenting his platoon.

He spoke as quickly as he could. The demons were catching up with him. He needed to wrap this up and get out of here ASAP.

"Any questions? No? That's good." Joe turned as if to leave when a dozen hands popped into the air.

If he hadn't been a Marine he would have groaned aloud. Showing no outward sign of his inner unrest, he pointed to the preadolescent boy near the back, one of the spitballers.

"Is it true that you saw aliens while you were up in the mountains?"

The bunch of very short recruits he'd been marooned with had indeed seemed like aliens to him, but he doubted that's what this preadolescent male meant. "Negative," Joe curtly replied. "I saw no indication of alien life-forms."

"Have you ever killed anybody?" the kid next to the spitballer demanded.

The roaring in Joe's ears escalated and he got tunnel

vision, the edges of the gymnasium turning black, as black as his soul.

"No more questions for now," Joe heard Prudence saying as if from a great distance. "Before Sergeant Wilder returns to the base, we'd like to give him a token of our appreciation." With a quick nod at her students, she indicated that they were to come forward now.

Keishon, Gem, Pete, Sinatra and Rosa held on to a large certificate that had obviously been created on the computer and then put together, somewhat inexpertly and unevenly, to include handwritten notes and drawings. This was no generic gift. This was one made from the heart.

Joe's eyes burned as he read what they'd written: "With appreciation to Sergeant Joe Wilder, our hero. From the sixth-grade students at Dixon Middle School."

Hero? Who was he kidding? He couldn't even stand in front of a bunch of rug rats and give a stupid speech without breaking into a cold sweat.

Drowning. He was drowning.

Closing his eyes, Joe flinched as images flashed through his mind. Terror. A small child. And him. For the first time Joe saw himself in the picture. Himself as a child, a four- or five-year-old watching his baby brother fall into the creek.

Save him, Joe, save him!

But he couldn't.

My God. He remembered. Remembered a past he'd been too young to really register. Until the helicopter crash. That crushing feeling of being to blame had dredged up those forgotten feelings from his earliest years.

This was why he freaked at being around kids. He was no hero. He never had been.

"I don't deserve this," Joe said roughly. "I didn't do anything to deserve it. Give the award to your teacher, she's much braver than I am." Saying that, he jammed his cover on his head and strode out of the gymnasium.

When Joe returned to base a short time later, he was greeted with the news that Sergeant Major Martin was looking for him.

Had his commanding officer heard about his abysmal performance at the middle school already? Joe was still trying to deal with the murky memories of his childhood, but there was no time for that now. He was on duty now. He was a Marine, by God. Not a kid.

The second Joe walked into the Sergeant Major's office, he knew he was in trouble. It was apparent in the gimlet stare he received, in the grave disapproval evident in his commanding officer's voice even as he barked, "At ease."

Joe did not relax. He remained standing, his posture cruise-missile straight, his hands clasped behind his back.

"I called you in here because I've been hearing some disturbing things, Sergeant. And I want to verify their veracity with you before I proceed any further."

Joe felt as if the white walls—decorated with framed photos of great moments in U.S. Marine Corps history, including the Marines raising the American flag at Iwo Jima—were closing in on him.

Had Prudence talked to her father after all? Clenching his jaw, Joe braced himself for whatever was to come.

"I heard the wildest rumor about you and my daughter."

Joe didn't say a word.

The Sergeant Major continued, "Now I'm saying this is a wild rumor because I fail to see how it could possibly be true. My daughter has too much sense and you're too good a Marine to disobey an order."

Actually the Sergeant Major had never ordered Joe not to kiss Prudence, but that was a mere technicality. Joe was well aware of the fact that his commanding officer wouldn't approve of his daughter and him locking lips.

"This wild rumor has it that you took my daughter bungee-jumping this weekend. True or false?" the Sergeant Major demanded.

This was about bungee-jumping? "False, sir. I did not take her bungee-jumping."

"I'm very glad to hear that. So my daughter did not go bungee-jumping. I knew she couldn't be that idiotic. But I needed to hear it from you. So just tell me that my daughter did not go bungee-jumping this weekend and I'll believe you."

Joe wanted to lie, but a lifetime of values wouldn't allow him to do that. A Marine was supposed to possess the highest of military virtues. A Marine never lies, cheats or compromises. He'd had that ingrained in him since birth.

"Sergeant. I asked you to tell me that my daughter did not go bungee-jumping this weekend."

"I can't tell you that, sir."

"Why not?"

"Because I'm afraid she did go bungee-jumping, sir."

Sergeant Major Martin pinned him with a steely-eyed glare. "Repeat that, Sergeant. Are you saying she did go bungee-jumping?"

"Affirmative, sir."

"Then how do you explain your previous answer regarding not taking her bungee-jumping." The Sergeant Major's voice lowered ominously.

"I did not *take* her bungee-jumping, sir," Joe clarified. "But she did bungee-jump."

"On her own? You weren't there?"

"I was there, sir. And I take full responsibility—"

"So you should," Sergeant Major Martin interrupted him to growl. "Are you insane? Allowing my daughter to risk her life?"

Joe didn't say anything in his own defense.

What was there to say? That yes he was afraid he might be going insane? That he'd been haunted by nightmares he couldn't make any sense out of until today? That he was driven crazy by desire for his commanding officer's incredibly sexy and infuriatingly stubborn daughter?

Yeah, right. All of that information was sure to go over real well. So he said nothing.

"I'm waiting for an answer, Sergeant."

"I'm sorry, sir," Joe said stiffly.

"Not half as sorry as you're going to be," Sergeant Major Martin declared ominously, his anger roaring in like a fast-moving storm front. "My daughter would never have done anything so...imprudent as bungee-jumping were it not for your influence on her. I'm holding you directly responsible for this uncharacteristic behavior on her part, and I'm hereby ordering you to stay away from my daughter!"

Chapter Eleven

Prudence had been trying to reach Joe all day on his cell phone and had left messages on his voice mail but he wasn't answering. She was worried about him. She'd never forget the tormented look on his face when he'd walked out of the school gymnasium yesterday. His eyes had held such a mixture of anguish and guilt that she'd hurt for him.

Her students had wondered if they'd said or done something wrong to make Joe leave so abruptly without the certificate they'd worked so hard on for him. She'd had a hard time explaining but had tried to ease their fears, telling them that just because Joe didn't feel he deserved to be called a hero didn't mean that he didn't merit the title. He *was* a hero, and she assured them that in time Joe would return to pick up his certificate.

"I think he's kinda shy," Rosa had said. "I don't think he liked speaking in front of everyone that way. I know I felt sick to my stomach when I had to give that oral book report last month and that was just in front of our own class not the entire school.''

''Did you tell him that I don't blame him for cutting those tree branches?'' Keishon had asked Prudence.

''I told him.''

''Maybe we could e-mail him,'' Sinatra had said. ''Send him a funny e-greeting card that would make him feel better.''

''I think he was upset that Pete misspelled the word Sergeant in his sign,'' Gem had said.

If only that were true. But Joe's demons went far deeper than a misspelled word or a case of public speaking jitters.

She'd seen his face go pale, the way he tried to hold himself together. Something had happened to him while he'd stood at that podium and she wouldn't rest until she found out what it was.

The only good news she'd gotten today was the return of her van. The last time she'd seen it was when she'd left it at the Sunshine Trailhead clearing on the other side of the state. Their backpacks had been returned earlier in the week, but her dad and a buddy of his had traveled over the weekend to get her van for her.

Pulling into her driveway, she was surprised to find her mom waiting for her. She was seated in the wicker rocking chair on the front porch, the one Prudence had given new life to by repainting it lime-green and adding a matching green gingham pillow.

Her mom's smile and wave assured Prudence that nothing was wrong.

''This is a surprise,'' Prudence said as she hurried up the steps, absently noting that the red geraniums would need watering sometime today. Their leaves were looking a little wilted.

That's how Prudence felt. A little wilted. Her yellow sleeveless cotton shirt clung to her back and her navy-blue slacks were badly wrinkled after a hectic day. It was hot and steamy, typical May weather for coastal North Carolina. Only a few more weeks and school would be out for the summer.

"I made us a pitcher of iced tea," her mom said.

"You're a lifesaver," Prudence murmured as she sank onto a plastic resin chair she'd slip-covered in a green gingham that matched the rocker's pillows.

"Have I told you what a great job you've done with this house, making it so cozy, so reflective of you?"

Prudence eyed her mom over the rim of her iced tea glass. "I have the feeling you didn't come here to compliment me about my decorating skills. What's up?"

Ellen sighed and rubbed away the condensation on her own tall glass before replying. "Your father has done something he shouldn't have, I'm afraid."

Prudence's stomach sank. "What do you mean?"

"Your father heard about you going bungee-jumping."

Prudence groaned. She'd meant to tell her parents about it herself, but hadn't been sure how to broach the subject. "I'll bet he went ballistic, huh?"

Her mother nodded. "I must say I was a bit surprised myself."

"I never meant to upset either one of you. It's just something that I had to do. And it really was an awesome experience, Mom!"

"I'll take your word for it. I just hope this isn't something you plan on doing a lot of?"

"I've been careful for a long time now," Prudence said quietly.

"I know you have, sweetie." Ellen patted her hand and gave her a knowing look the way only a mother could. "Ever since that car accident you've been trying to make up for something, trying to prove something. I know that."

"I went a little overboard on the caution thing."

"You always were an all-or-nothing kind of child," Ellen noted with a grin. "No half measures for you."

"I know. But I realized I'd become so afraid to take any kind of risk, emotional or otherwise, that I'd wrapped myself in a cocoon and wasn't experiencing life the way I could be. Being snowbound up in the mountains with Joe made me realize that."

"Well, it turns out your father had a bit of a run-in with your Joe," Ellen admitted.

"But Joe had nothing to do with my bungee-jumping," Prudence said. "Well, he did have something to do with it—he helped me realize that I'd been trying so hard not to do anything wrong, to play it safe that I'd just about stopped living. But he was totally against me jumping. In fact, he ordered me not to."

"I have to confess that I wasn't real fond of the idea of my daughter leaping off some tower in a daredevil stunt," Ellen said. "But I also have to confess that a part of me was glad that you were finally back to your old self. We haven't really talked about it, but I know that after the car accident you did everything in your power not to make any waves, to be careful and not make any mistakes. But as you said, you took it to such extremes that you weren't experiencing all life has to offer. That's not to say that I think you should be doing more daredevil stuff. I'd rather not have any more white hair than I've already got, if you don't mind.''

"What did Dad say to Joe?"

"I'm not sure exactly what he said. You know how your father is. But I do know that yesterday he ordered Joe not to see you anymore."

Prudence's heart stopped. "How could he do that?"

"Very easily in the heat of the moment I suspect."

"He's going to ruin everything!" Prudence cried, leaping to her feet.

"What do you mean?"

"I'm in love with Joe Wilder, Mom."

"And is he in love with you?"

"He might be."

Her mother raised an eyebrow. "Might be?"

"He has a hard time talking about his feelings right now, and Dad certainly made things worse by ordering Joe not to see me. Joe lives and breathes the Marine Corps. He'd never disobey an order." Prudence set down her glass so abruptly that iced tea sloshed over the top. "I can't believe Dad did that!"

"He's worried about you. And so am I. Not because of the bungee-jumping, but because of you loving a man who may or may not love you back. Sweetie, did something happen when the two of you were alone that night up in the mountains? I never asked you…"

"Joe was a perfect gentleman," Prudence stated.

Her mother heaved a sigh of relief.

"I didn't want him to be, though," Prudence said.

"Oh, sweetie." Her look was a woman-to-woman expression of acknowledgment that her daughter was a grown woman now.

"I love him, Mom."

"Being snowbound in the mountains, fighting the

elements the way you two did, well it's bound to make a special bond. But once you return to real life—''

"Joe tried saying the same thing," Prudence interrupted her.

"And you didn't believe him?"

"There are things I can't say, things he told me. Just trust me, Mom, when I say that Joe understands me, and I understand him. And when we're together, it's like the Fourth of July and Christmas all wrapped into one. Fireworks and anticipation. Magic.''

Ellen looked worried. "This has just happened all so fast...."

"I think I fell a little bit in love with him when I was eight and he was ten. We connected back then, and although I'm the first to admit that the sparks flew when we met again, I fell in love with him again. Believe me, I didn't want to love him. He's a Marine. I didn't want anything to do with another military man, not after Steven humiliated me. And any other Marine I've ever dated has gotten called onto to the carpet by Dad. I just can't believe he's done it again. Where is he?" she demanded.

"He was feeling out of sorts, so he said he was going to try to squeeze in some fishing in at his favorite spot before it got dark. Where are you going?" Ellen asked as Prudence headed to her van.

"To go tell my father that I'm not his little princess anymore and it's time he stopped treating me like one!"

Prudence was so riled up it was amazing she didn't get a speeding ticket as she headed out to her father's fishing hole. She hadn't even taken the time to change clothes, but had hopped right into her van and driven out to confront him.

Dust clung to her van and to her slacks by the time she'd traveled down the gravel side road and hiked the dirt trail to his special spot. And there he was, calmly fishing as if he hadn't just messed up her life.

"How could you?" she angrily shouted, clearly startling him with both her presence and her fury.

"Blast it, princess, you almost made me drop my fishing rod!" he growled, glaring at her under the brim of his battered good-luck fishing hat. "What are you doing here?"

"I came to talk to you."

"I'm fishing," he said, returning his attention to his fishing line.

"Forget fishing," she growled, tugging on his arm and almost making him drop his rod again. When he was facing her, she said, "How could you order Joe not to see me?"

He sighed and set his rod aside. "So that's what this is about."

"Yes, that's what this is about."

"I suppose your mother told you."

"Yes, she told me that you made an absolute fool of yourself. Oh, don't go giving me that look. Like Marines never make fools of themselves." She rolled her eyes. "Please!"

"I did not make a fool of myself," he said stiffly. "The man took you bungee-jumping."

"He did not *take* me," she instantly corrected him. "Joe tried to stop me. In fact, he ordered me not to jump. Did he tell you that?"

"No."

"Did you give him the chance?"

Her father gave her an offended look. "Of course, I gave him the chance. He said he took full responsibility."

"He's so full of…hooey!" she said in exasperation. "He is *not* responsible. Any more than he was responsible for the blizzard. Unless you plan on blaming him for that, too?"

"Of course not. The man saved your life."

"And this is how you repaid him?" she demanded.

"I'd just found out my only child had jumped off a bridge."

"I didn't jump off a bridge, I jumped from a tower specially designed for bungee-jumping."

He held out a hand in a clear order for her to stop. "I don't want to hear the details."

"No, you just want to jump to incorrect conclusions. Don't confuse you with facts, you already know what you think."

He eyed her cautiously. "I've never seen you this upset."

"I'm furious with you!"

"Sergeant Wilder never said a word in his defense…."

"He'd never do that," Prudence said. "Joe doesn't feel he deserves to be happy."

Her father frowned. "Why not?"

She looked away. "He has his reasons."

"Well, how was I supposed to know that?"

"You could have come to me first, asking me about the bungee-jumping instead of going to Joe behind my back."

"He's in my command," he growled. "I've got the right to question him."

She stood her ground. "Not about his private life and mine."

"I'm not going to stand here and argue with you," he said, reaching for his fishing rod again. "You're scaring away all the fish. I came here to get some peace and quiet after a rough day."

"You came here because you feel guilty about what you did today."

"Oh, so now you're a mind reader? What?" he demanded as her eyes teared up. "What did I say?"

"Joe said that to me." Her voice was unsteady. "For a minute there you sounded just like him."

"Aw jeez." He patted her shoulder awkwardly. "Maybe you should go talk to your mother about this."

"No, I'm going to go talk to Joe about this."

"He's a fine Marine, princess. He won't disobey a direct order from his commanding officer, and I ordered him not to see you."

"Then you'll just have to rescind that order," she said, glaring at her father, daring him to contradict her. "But first I have to find him."

"Why do you do it, Wilder?" The question was repeated by a half dozen of his fellow Marines seated around a battered wooden table in The American Bar. The place was one of many local hangouts for Marines.

"Why? For the thrill," Joe replied, wiping away the condensation forming on his icy-cold bottle of beer before taking several more healthy swigs.

"Forget why, *how* do you do it?" the guy next to Joe asked in amazement. "You get me even near a helo and I start to hurl."

Rotor blades gleaming, flames shooting skyward. *Don't go there....*

Willing the darkness away, Joe quickly finished off his beer and reached for another.

"I can't imagine bungee-jumping," the guy continued. "How do you do it, Wilder?"

That was the million-dollar question, wasn't it? Joe cynically thought to himself. How did he do it? How did he manage to convince dozens of fellow Marines, not to mention his superior officers, that he was a fearless daredevil who loved spending his off-duty hours bungee-jumping or tearing around on his Harley motorcycle or white-water kayaking alone in water so wild it seemed as if no one could make it through alive.

Alive. The risk-taking had always made him feel alive. Until he'd seen Prudence taking that "leap of faith" as she'd called it. Then he'd felt as if he was going to die. And now his commanding officer had not only ordered him to stop bungee-jumping, but he'd ordered Joe to stay away from Prudence.

Which was just what he deserved.

Now he wasn't able to prove his courage by constantly testing the limits of his endurance. There was no point. Joe knew the truth. He was no hero.

"He's not revealing any secrets," the guy to his right said with a laugh. McCormick was his name. Joe only knew that because it was written in stencils on the man's uniform pocket. These men weren't his close buddies, but they were Marines and that made them his *compadres* tonight.

McCormick was right. Joe wasn't about to reveal any secrets. And it turned out he had plenty—dark secrets he'd blocked from his own memory until now. He finished one bottle of beer and reached for another.

"Come on, Wilder, give us a few tips. I've heard you've got a real way with women."

"You heard right. Look at the way Lucy hung all over him when she was serving our drinks," the African-American guy on his left said. Joe squinted to read his name in the increasingly smoky interior of the bar. Or maybe it was his vision making things blurry. Too much beer and not enough sleep had never been a good combination.

"Come on, Wilder, tell us how you do it," McCormick said.

By not giving a damn. By giving too many damns. By blocking out the memories. By reliving them vividly in his dreams every night.

How did he do it? How did he survive knowing that the only reason he was alive right now was that another Marine had died in his place? How did he survive knowing that he'd failed even at a young age with fatal results?

He had no idea. Distracting the guys with the promise to buy them all another round of beer, Joe smiled and cracked jokes while inside he felt himself sinking deeper into an abyss he saw no way out of.

"Hey, Danny!" a woman at the next table shouted to someone out of sight.

Joe felt the blood drain from his face as he flashed back to that nightmarish day so long ago—the water, a young child, terror. His voice. Yelling Danny. His brother's name had been Danny!

Reality hit him like a land mine.

He needed more alcohol. Turning to order another round of beers, he saw Prudence.

"Hey look, there's another stunning babe eyeing you, Wilder," McCormick said from beside him.

"That's Sergeant Major Martin's daughter," Joe growled.

McCormick gulped.

"I've been looking all over for you, Joe," Prudence said as she joined them, looking rumpled and completely out of place in her schoolteacher blouse and slacks. Looking sexy as hell. "We need to talk."

Joe recognized that stubborn look on her face. She wasn't going to be turned away easily. Fine. Nothing about this damn day had been easy.

"Can we go someplace else, someplace quieter?" she asked.

He sipped more beer before answering her. "No."

She sighed as if he were one of her difficult students. "Then can we at least go sit at a table together?"

Joe shook his head, which made the room spin. "I don't think that's a good idea."

"What do you say, guys?" This time Prudence aimed her request at the other Marines at the table. "Can you give the two of us a little privacy here?"

They scattered like pigeons.

But then she was a Sergeant Major's daughter. Smart guys. Dumb him.

"I'm sorry, Joe," she said, sitting down and pulling her chair closer so that she could speak to him above the noise of a Garth Brooks song blaring over the bar's sound system. "I'm so sorry my father threw a hissy fit yesterday. He shouldn't have done that."

Joe almost choked on his beer. A Sergeant Major? Throwing a hissy fit?

Unaware or uncaring of her breach of military etiquette, she continued. "He should never have ordered you to stay away from me. That was very wrong of him."

"He was dead right." Joe's laugh was harsh and bitter. "You're better off without me."

"Why?" she demanded. "Because of the helo accident? You're not to blame for that."

He'd heard it all before. She didn't know the rest of the story, the ugly truth he'd just discovered about himself. It was time he told her. "But I am to blame for my baby brother's death."

His words shocked her. "Wha...at?"

"That's why I get the shakes around kids," he said in a flat voice, his face devoid of emotion. "You noticed it right off."

"I noticed you weren't real comfortable around my students at first."

"Not real comfortable?" His laughter was harsh and bitter. "Try scared out of my mind. Same thing at the cabin. It got worse there. The thing was, I couldn't figure out why. I'd never had a problem dealing with kids before. But I realized yesterday at that school thing that the helo accident had dredged up something from my past."

"What happened?" Her voice was quiet, her warm brown eyes gazing at him with sympathy and compassion instead of revulsion.

Joe had to look away. He didn't deserve all the things she was offering him. "My baby brother drowned and I didn't save him, that's what happened." His hard words contrasted with her softness as he fought the rising emotion clawing at his chest, making it hard for him to breathe. "His name was

Danny. I'd forgotten that. Forgotten him, can you believe that?''

"How old were you when this happened?"

Her continued questions stabbed at him, making him shudder with the effort to keep himself under control. "I don't know," he said impatiently. "Four, maybe."

"Practically a baby yourself. So a baby like you was supposed to somehow save your younger brother, is that the scenario you've set up for yourself? Where were your parents?"

Frowning, Joe rubbed his forehead. "I don't remember. My family never talked about it. I didn't even remember it until yesterday."

Instead of backing away, she moved closer, putting her arm around his taut shoulders. "It's not unusual for a traumatic experience to bring back similar memories. And if you don't believe me, then you should talk to someone else about this. Your family, a close friend, or I can recommend someone."

"A shrink?" He jerked away from her. "Forget it."

"I can't forget it because you can't forget. The survivor guilt is eating you up inside, Joe. Part of you wants to die, too. You think I don't know that?" she said with gritty sincerity. "Do you think I didn't feel that way after my mom was hurt so badly? I did. But I got help."

"You're not a Marine" was his low slicing reply. "A Marine doesn't need help."

"What about love, Joe?" She faced him without fear, letting him see her love for him in her eyes and in her voice, baring her soul to him. "Does a Marine need love?"

Joe couldn't tell her. Couldn't let her see into the

pitch-black darkness of his heart. Was she stupid? Couldn't she see how unworthy he was of her love? What would it take to get that message through her head?

Joe knew the answer to that and he acted on that knowledge, sloughing off her words with a dismissive shrug and a mocking smile. "You think I'm not getting enough love? Think again, honey." He snagged a willing barmaid in his free arm and tugged her onto his lap. "Hey, Lucy, tell my commanding officer's princess of a daughter here that I've got enough love."

"Don't you worry about him," Lucy purred, stroking Joe's chest with her hands.

"Hear that?" Joe tossed a look of utter indifference toward Prudence before issuing her a curt order. "Stop following me, stop flirting with me. I'm not interested, okay? I'm not alone and I'm certainly not in need of love, so just leave me alone. What does it take to get through to you?"

Prudence sat like a block of ice, unable to believe what she was seeing or hearing. Why? Why was he doing this to her?

"Go away!" Joe bluntly growled, his blue eyes filled with fire. "Not you, honey," he muttered to the barmaid on his lap, draping her arms around his neck. "You stay right where you are."

"Glad to," Lucy drawled, leaning forward to kiss him.

Joe kissed her back.

Realizing she'd lost her bid to save him from himself, Prudence stood so quickly she almost overturned the chair.

Who was she kidding? Joe didn't need saving. She'd projected her own feelings onto him. She was nothing but a bother to him. How could she have been so wrong, so blind? She had to get out of there.

Keeping her head held high as she walked out of the bar prevented the scalding tears filling her eyes from spilling down her cheeks. Rejection. Humiliation.

This is what she got for being bold and taking risks—her heart stomped into itty-bitty pieces by a lean, mean Marine.

Chapter Twelve

Seeing the bruised pain in Prudence's eyes had nearly brought Joe to his knees. He'd almost dumped Lucy off his lap and chased after Prudence before common sense reasserted itself.

"Oh, babe, you've got it bad," Lucy the barmaid said, sympathetically patting his cheek. "You're in love with that girl."

"Sorry, Lucy," he said with an apologetic half smile.

"Not as sorry as you're going to be if you don't go after her," Lucy replied, hopping off his lap to give him a challenging look.

"I can't do that."

Lucy just shook her head in the way of one who'd had her share of heartbreak and headed back to the bar.

He'd done the right thing in sending Prudence away, Joe reminded himself. She was better off without him. It would get easier as time went on.

But by Friday, as his nightmares intensified, Joe realized that things couldn't continue on the way they were. He had to do something.

Know your enemy. A Marine Corps rule. Joe's enemy was the guilt and the fear. He had to dig deeper, he had to own it and overcome it. Or he'd never get over it.

One thing Prudence had said was right on the money. He needed to talk to someone. And deep in his heart, Joe knew who that someone needed to be. He needed to call his dad.

Joe's hands were sweating as he pushed the speed-dial button programmed into his cell phone. As soon as his weekend liberty had started he'd driven his Jeep out onto a deserted stretch of coastal road, so that no one would see or hear him if he broke down while making this call.

No, that wasn't an option, Joe fiercely reminded himself. He couldn't break down. His dad would be so ashamed of him. Bill Wilder valued strength and integrity in his sons.

Doubts filled Joe's head, making his stomach burn. *Maybe I should call one of my brothers instead.*

He was about to hang up when his dad answered. "Hello?"

The sound of his dad's bellowing, gravelly voice steadied his nerves. "Hey, Dad. It's Joe." Closing his eyes, he could easily picture his father. Similar in height and stature to Sergeant Major Martin, his dad had a grunt rifleman's demeanor and the inquiring mind of a self-taught intellectual. He also had blue eyes and a wicked sense of humor—both traits inherited by all his sons. He just recently retired after thirty years in the Marine Corps.

"Hey, how's it going, son?"

"Not so good," Joe admitted, unable to keep up any pretense of small talk even for a short while. "I don't know how to bring this up…"

"We're Marines, son. You don't have to go stepping on eggshells around me."

"It's about Danny." The words came out in a rush, then Joe's mouth dried up and he couldn't speak.

The utter silence on the other end of the phone line told him that his dad was shocked. His dad was rarely at a loss for words.

"I'm sorry." Joe's voice was harsh and unsteady.

"I didn't think you remembered anything about Danny." His dad's voice sounded just as shredded as his.

Slowly at first, in a jumbled tangle of half sentences, Joe told him about the helicopter accident and his feelings of guilt and how that had triggered his panicked reaction to kids, which had in turn finally triggered his repressed memory about Danny. He ended by whispering, "I didn't save him, Dad."

"Save him?" his father repeated. "Joe, you were just a little kid. I was the parent. I was the one who should have been looking after you both. For God's sake, I'm the one who should be filled with guilt, not you. I never talked about it, the family never talked about it. That was my decision. It was probably the wrong decision, I can see that now. But I was so consumed with guilt that I couldn't stand to talk about it, so I locked it up. My baby son drowned on my watch. My fault. No excuses, no exceptions."

Joe was stunned to find that his dad, his infallible dad felt guilty.

"What? You thought you were the only one to ever experience guilt?" his dad asked.

"No," Joe replied, thinking of Prudence. "How did you recover?"

"You don't so much recover as you continue on. You can't allow the regrets and the guilt to do you in. You can't go down that road, son."

"Too late. I've already halfway down that road," Joe replied.

"Then about-face!" his dad barked like the drill sergeant he'd once been. "Turn around right now, before it's too late." His voice softened and vibrated with intensity as he continued, "Listen to me, son. Accidents happen. It isn't fair, it isn't right. Danny's drowning was an accident. The ground just gave way next to that creekbed. I've relived that moment over and over again in my head. If only I'd gotten to him faster, if only I'd kept him further away from the creek."

"Yeah," Joe agreed huskily. "Those 'if only's' are tough."

"Not as tough as you are. Remember that. What doesn't destroy you strengthens you. Don't let this destroy you, Joe. Danny wouldn't want that. Those guys on that helo wouldn't want that and I sure as hell don't want that. Understood?"

"Yes, sir."

Joe had just hung up when his cell phone rang again. Stupid as it was, he thought it might be Prudence. Which was *really* stupid. After the way he'd treated her, she'd never come near him again.

Instead the caller was Curt. "Where are you?" he demanded.

"In my Jeep," Joe replied. "Where are you?"

"In a motel room ten minutes from Camp Lejeune."

"You're kidding, right?"

"You're the kidder in life, not me. I'm the brooding loner type, remember?"

"That was your past life," Joe heard Jessie saying in the background.

"The whole family is here," Curt said.

"What are you doing down here?"

"We suddenly felt the need for some North Carolina sunshine."

Joe's grunt of disbelief made his opinion of that statement clear.

"Not buying that, huh?" Curt noted dryly. "Well, I've got this buddy who sounded like he needed my help, so here I am. Are you coming over or do I have to track you down, devil dog?"

"I'll be right over."

"I can't believe you did this!" Curt was waiting for him outside of the small motel unit. Joe walked over and slapped him on the back in a macho version of a hug that expressed emotion without getting sappy.

Curt responded in kind, fiercely thumping Joe's back before stepping away. Curt's limp, a result of a sniper attack in Bosnia a little over two years ago, was still visible, although not as much as it once had been. "I couldn't stay away."

"You really didn't have to…"

Curt whacked Joe's back again. "I know."

"Where's the rest of the family?"

"Inside," Curt replied. "I thought I'd meet you out here in case seeing Blue made you uncomfortable or anything."

Joe took the opportunity to fill Curt in on what had transpired over the past week.

"Man, that's a lot to deal with," Curt quietly acknowledged. "You think you can do what your father ordered? Turn back from that road to guilt?"

Before Joe could answer, the motel room door opened and Blue wailed, *"Daaaddddeee!"*

"I'm right here, Blue. Daddy loves you, but I'm busy right now. Go on and get back inside now. I'll be there in a little while."

"It's okay," Joe said, sounding a bit surprised by the realization. "I want to see Blue."

"Are you sure?" Curt asked.

"Yeah, I am."

Curt's little girl had grown since the last time Joe had seen her but she was still cute as a button. She had brown eyes. Like Prudence. Joe's heart ached but the raw panic was gone.

"Who's this gorgeous little girl?" Joe demanded.

"It's me, Blue, Uncle Joe. Don't you remember me?"

His heart ached some more. Blue was looking up at him with such hopeful anticipation. Prudence had looked at him the same way, only with a woman's passion and compassion.

"I think I screwed up big-time," Joe muttered as the truth hit him. He was in love with Prudence Martin. Whether he deserved her or not was another question. He had some things to prove to himself first.

"That's okay," Blue assured Joe, patting his arm with her small five-year-old hand still sticky with the remnants of a cherry lollipop she had in her other fist. "My daddy screws up big-time sometimes, too.

Mommy loves him anyway and so do I. We love you, too, Uncle Joe, even if you do screw up."

Man, talk about a power punch to the heart.

Joe had to blink away the tears. Scooping Blue up, he hugged her to him in a way his fellow Marines would no doubt think was downright sappy. He didn't care, and neither did Blue who happily hugged him back.

It wasn't until Joe heard Curt's chuckle that he realized that Blue's lollipop was now stuck to his nape.

"Thanks, kiddo," Joe told Blue before setting her down and removing the offending lollipop. "I love you, too. Even if you have a father with a twisted sense of humor," he added darkly with a warning look in Curt's direction.

His buddy appeared totally unrepentant. Perhaps that had something to do with the fact that Curt was standing there with his wife Jessie in his arms, clearly a happy camper. "I seem to recall a certain instance where you laughed at me when I had happy face stickers stuck to the sole of my shoes," Curt reminded him.

"I'm not allowed to put stickers on Daddy's Marine things anymore," Blue solemnly declared. "They can only go in my sticker book. Want to see?"

"Sure. Jessie, have you grown tired of this devil dog yet?"

"Never," Jessie replied with a loving smile. Moving forward she engulfed Joe in a friendly hug. "It's good to see you, Joe."

"I can't believe you guys came all the way down here."

Her green eyes were warm with understanding. "We wanted to."

"You still a preschool teacher?"

Jessie nodded, her blond hair bouncing against her shoulders. "That's right."

"We seem to share a thing for schoolteachers," Joe told Curt.

"As long as it's not the same schoolteacher," Curt replied, snagging his wife in his arms and kissing her.

Joe was willing to bet a year's salary that Jessie and Prudence would get along. While Jessie was a blonde and Prudence had darker hair, both women possessed a warm and giving nature that went beyond surface beauty. And both women possessed a combination of practical femininity that didn't need layers of makeup and red-hot lipstick to make them sexy.

Later, after Joe had carefully gone over all of Blue's sticker books with her and read her several stories—including her favorite, *The Wishing Tree*—he got a chance to talk alone with Jessie while Curt tucked Blue in.

They were just outside the motel room, sitting at a wooden picnic table and drinking sodas. Joe had felt it only fair to give her an abbreviated explanation of what was going on with him.

Her gentle smile told him she understood. "One of the ironies of the healing process is that you have to delve into the past in order to put it behind you," she said. "I had to do that, about my past with Curt going back to our high school days. It sounds like you've done that with your father today."

"Yeah, I did. And being with Blue today…well, I didn't panic once."

"I'm glad, Joe."

When Curt came out, Jessie returned to the motel room to give the two men some privacy.

"So, Wilder, you said earlier that you'd screwed up," Curt noted. "Care to elaborate?"

"Not really."

"I can probably guess." Narrowing his eyes, Curt fixed him with a speculative look. "Let's see…you somehow did something stupid or rotten or both to scare Prudence away, thereby accomplishing the goal of your commanding officer's order of not seeing his daughter again while simultaneously making sure that she didn't get too close to you so that you could keep your own personal perimeter wall in place. Affirmative?"

Joe nodded before grudgingly admitting, "Damn, you're good."

Grinning, Curt shrugged and said, "Yeah, well, I've had some help over the years."

"Hindsight is twenty-twenty, isn't that how that phrase goes? You know all that extreme sport stuff— the bungee-jumping and the kayaking and the bike racing—it was all a way to prove my courage over and over again."

"Courage isn't the absence of fear, it's the strength to overcome fear," Curt quietly said. "Do you really still wish it was you that went down in that helo? Because I, for one, am damn glad it wasn't. Instead of this guilt stuff you should be looking at this as a second chance. And God knows those don't come around very often. I'm speaking from experience here. I got a second chance at a life with Jessie and I'm grateful for that every hour of every day. Don't blow your second chance, Wilder. Don't blow it."

Prudence was kneeling in her small back garden, yanking out weeds with a vengeance when her portable phone rang from the white resin table nearby. Shoving her sweaty hair out of her face, she tugged off her ladybug gardening gloves and picked up the phone, only then realizing she'd just smeared dirt all over her forehead. "Hello?" She sounded like the Wicked Witch of the West.

"Prudence, is that you? It's Vanessa. I just got the birthday packet you sent. Thank you so much."

Gratefully sinking into a lawn chair, Prudence had to smile at her friend's enthusiasm. At the moment Princess Vanessa Alexandria Maria Teresa Von Volzemburg sounded like a kid instead of European royalty. "I'm glad you liked it. I thought every princess should have her own rubber ducky."

"I've always thought so," Vanessa agreed, "but for some reason there wasn't a rubber ducky to be found in the entire castle until you were kind enough to send me a pair of them."

"I sent you two because I didn't want one to get lonely on its own."

"You're sounding rather lonely yourself at the moment," Vanessa noted with concern. "Is something wrong?"

"I don't want to ruin your birthday by raining on your parade," Prudence replied.

"Here in Volzemburg the sun always shines and we always have perfect weather."

She laughed. "I thought that was in Camelot."

"My father wants to turn our country into the equivalent of Camelot."

"That's a good thing, right?"

"Not when he wants to do his Merlin thing and try to turn me into something I'm not," Vanessa muttered. "But enough about me. Tell me what's wrong? Is it a man?"

"What makes you say that?" Prudence demanded.

"Feminine intuition."

"Well, it's not just a man," Prudence said. "It's a Marine."

"Oh my, that's much worse, isn't it."

"You've got that right." Prudence could feel the tears, always close at bay these days, welling again. She'd already cried buckets over Joe Wilder. He wasn't worth one more tear. Not one.

"Tell me again why Marines are worse than men?" Vanessa prompted her.

"Because they think they're better at everything." Prudence sniffed and reached for a Kleenex. "I'm not crying," she informed Vanessa. "I've got allergies."

"I suspect you're allergic to Marines," her friend noted ruefully.

"I'm *definitely* allergic to Marines. But that didn't seem to stop me from falling in love with one."

"Oh my." Vanessa's voice was filled with sympathy. "What happened?"

"He doesn't feel the same way about me at all."

"How do you know?"

"Well, maybe it was the fact that he flat out told me to go away and stop bothering him. Or maybe it was the fact that he was kissing another woman when he told me that."

"That doesn't sound good," Vanessa agreed.

Prudence laughed unsteadily. "Still the mistress of understatements, I see."

"Yes, well, it wouldn't do for me to get too dramatic now, would it? Not very princessy of me. Tell me, does this Marine have a name?"

"Yes. Joe Wilder."

"Ah. Well, I suppose it's just as well that things didn't work out. I mean think of this—if you'd have married the man your married name would have been Prudence Wilder. Think how conflicted you'd be—the prudent side of you versus the wilder side."

Prudence had to smile. "Only you could cheer me up on a day like today," she said. "I should have seen disaster coming. I mean, you'd think I'd learn. Each time I do something reckless, someone gets hurt. When I was a teenager, it was my mom in the car accident. And when I decided to go after Joe, I ended up making a fool of myself and getting my heart broken. At least nothing went wrong when I went bungee-jumping—"

"Back up a moment, please," Vanessa interrupted her to request. "What's this about bungee-jumping?"

"I finally did it last week."

"You lucky girl, you." There was a real sense of envy in her friend's voice. "I wish I could do something wild like that," Vanessa added wistfully.

"Why can't you? You're a princess, you can do anything you want."

"I can't *because* I'm a princess. My father would have a fit."

"Hey, your father may be a king, but you are still an American citizen." Since Vanessa's mother had been an American citizen and had actually returned to New York City to give birth because of medical complications, Vanessa had dual citizenship with America and Volzemburg. Aside from her time in a New England boarding school with Prudence, Vanessa had spent most of her life in Volzemburg with her widowed father and younger sister. "You could always give it all up and come live the life of a regular citizen here in good ol' U.S.A."

"Don't think there aren't times when I'm tempted," Vanessa replied before changing the subject. "I wish there was something I could do to make you feel better. Shall I send you more chocolate from the royal chocolatier?"

"They were delicious," Prudence admitted, "but the last time you did that I gained ten pounds."

"Volzemburg is known for its chocolate," Vanessa noted proudly.

"You're the one celebrating a birthday. I should be sending you chocolate."

"I can get the best chocolate in the world anytime I like. But you sent me a pair of rubber duckies and a carton of my favorite White Cat popcorn. Trust me, I'm in *your* debt."

"No, I'm in yours. You cheered me up when I really needed it. Thanks, Vanessa. Thanks for being there for me."

"You've always been there for me. Any Marine who doesn't appreciate what a special person you are should be tossed in the dungeon. We've still got one here at St. Kristoff Castle."

"Thanks for the offer. I'll keep it in mind should I ever run into Joe again. But I don't think that's going to happen. I *will* get over him," Prudence vowed.

"I hope you do. But if that doesn't happen, keep my dungeon in mind," Vanessa added with her irrepressible humor.

"I will," Prudence agreed, laughing through her tears.

* * *

"Sergeant Wilder, this is a surprise." Sergeant Major Martin looked at him with the impassive face of a fine poker player. Or a fine Marine.

But Joe was no slouch in the poker or Marine department himself. He no longer felt the office walls were closing in on him, no longer felt intimidated by the framed photos of great moments in U.S. Marine Corps history. Because he was a part of that history. "Permission to speak freely, sir."

"Granted."

Joe saw no point in beating around the bush here. "In that case, sir, I feel it only fair to inform you that I love your daughter and I intend to ask her to marry me at the soonest opportunity."

A good warrior prepared himself for several possible responses from an opponent. Joe had done that. He had his arguments ready for anything Sergeant Major Martin might throw at him. Except for these words. "Well, it certainly took you long enough."

Joe couldn't trust his ears. "Excuse me, sir?"

The Sergeant Major clapped him on the back in a congratulatory manner. "I thought I'd never see you two settle down together."

"Sir?"

"Why else do you think I assigned you to go with Prudence up into the mountains?"

"I don't understand. The other day you forbade me from seeing Prudence."

"That bungee-jumping episode rattled me," the other man admitted. "Besides, it wouldn't do to make things too easy for you, now would it? Now all you have to do is speak to my daughter. Permission granted to do so. Dismissed, Sergeant. And good luck."

"Thank you, sir. I have a feeling I may well need it." Joe had the feeling that Prudence hadn't told her father about Joe's behavior in the bar or the older man wouldn't be as confident as he appeared to be.

"You're a good Marine, Sergeant. I have every confidence in your abilities. Well, what are you doing still standing here, Wilder? Go propose to my daughter. Sweep her off her feet if you have to. Just don't take her bungee-jumping again or I'll have to tear your devil dog heart out. Understood?"

"Yes, sir."

Unable to wait until she got home from work, Joe returned to her school, the site of his last major panic attack. Classes were over but apparently only recently so because there were still plenty of kids milling around—waiting for school buses, gathering in little groups for the walk home.

He could tell which kids were from Prudence's class because they were the ones who gave him dirty looks. Outside the door to her classroom he ran into a wall of solid defense in the shape of Gem, Pete, Keishon and Rosa. Even Sinatra was there, although he did give Joe a sympathetic look even as he took his place beside Gem.

"You can't go in there," Keishon stated firmly. She was wearing her I'm Mean and Green T-shirt again and clearly meant business.

Joe tried to charm her with his smile.

The kid wasn't having any of it.

"Why can't I go in there?"

"Because outsiders aren't allowed in the school without a pass from the principal."

"I didn't have a pass last time I was here."

"You were an invited guest then." Her implication was clear. He wasn't welcome now.

"Look, if this is about my turning down that great gift you guys made for me..."

"We're not lame enough to be upset about that," Gem said.

"Then what's this about?"

"You bummed out Ms. Martin," Pete said. "We've tried to cheer her up but nothing worked, not even flowers from Rosa's mom's garden."

"And they were really nice flowers," Rosa added. "My mom's best roses."

"Sinatra even brought chocolate."

"It was just Hershey's kisses, but usually they make Ms. Martin smile," Sinatra said, giving Joe an accusing look. "Not this time, though."

"Look, I'm here to make things up with Prudence. But you guys are getting in the way."

"We don't want you hurting her again," Keishon said, standing firm.

How could a Marine like him not admire their loyalty?

"I'm not here to hurt her," he assured them. "I'm here to sweep her off her feet."

"Like you did getting us into that helicopter that rescued us?"

"Well, I am here to rescue Prudence." Rescue her from his own stupidity and make things up to her. He had to get into that classroom before she saw him out here and did something rash, like call security on him. "Look, I'm here to ask her to marry me."

"You're not even wearing your dress blues," Rosa noted with disapproval. "You looked better in your dress blues."

"Green is my favorite color," Keishon said in his defense. "That's the outfit he was wearing when he first met Ms. Martin at the base," she added.

"It's a uniform, not an outfit," Sinatra corrected her. "Marines don't wear outfits, right sir?"

"That's right, Sinatra. Now I could use your help in this operation."

Five pairs of curious kids' eyes focused on him. Funny that now he could think of them as the kids they truly were.

"Think the five of you are up to it?"

"Not if you're going to get us into trouble," the practical Gem replied.

"All you have to do is step away from the door and not do anything while I sweep your teacher off her feet."

Joe was hoping he could do that sweeping by talking to Prudence but the minute he saw her face, he knew that wouldn't work.

First her brown eyes widened with surprise, then they heated up with fury.

"Get out of my classroom!" Prudence growled, advancing on him with unmistakable warning. "You've got three seconds and I'm calling in security."

No, she definitely wasn't in the mood to listen to any explanations from him, let alone a declaration of love. Desperate action was clearly required. And fast.

"A good plan violently executed now is better than a perfect plan executed later," he told her before tugging her closer and efficiently executing a fireman's lift that had her dangling over his shoulder. She was not a happy camper, pounding on his back with her clenched fists and squirming like a beached fish.

He clamped his hand over her bottom, noting as he did so that she was wearing that black skirt he'd liked so much the last time he'd visited the school. Her sandals slid off her feet and she threatened him with all kinds of bodily harm as he strode out of the school with her.

"It's okay, Ms. Martin," Rosa called out reassuringly. "He's just sweeping you off your feet so he can propose."

She froze. He took advantage of her temporary impassivity to put her into his Jeep, which he'd left running. A second later they'd left the school behind, with Rosa, Gem, Keishon, Pete and Sinatra shouting encouragement like the bridal party in a wedding. All they were missing was the rice.

"How could you lie to those children?" Prudence demanded, staring back at them.

"I wasn't lying."

"I'm giving you one last chance to stop this Jeep."

"Can't do that."

"My father is going to have you court-martialed for this."

"I don't care."

His words stunned her.

"Where are you taking me?"

"You'll see." He took her to the deserted parking lot of the bungee-jumping tower. The place was closed on Mondays so they were the only ones there.

Opening the door for her, he motioned her over to the stand of palmetto palms where they'd had their last confrontation. "Why did you bring me here? The last time I saw you, you ordered me to stop bothering you."

"That would be impossible," he said huskily, practically eating her up with his blue eyes. "You've bothered me from the moment I saw you at the base.

You've gotten to me in a way no other woman ever has.''

Prudence couldn't believe him, as much as she wanted to. He'd hurt her too badly. She had to hang on to her anger, had to wrap it around her like an armored blanket to protect her from his charming ways. "You think you can storm back into my life and sweep me off my feet and sweet-talk me? Well, Sergeant, it's not going to work. You told me to go away and I went. Now I'm telling you to go away.''

"I'm not going anyplace. I'm so sorry," Joe whispered, cupping her face with his hand. "I'm so sorry I hurt you.''

She blinked away the tears. Marines hardly ever apologized. And she'd certainly never had a man look at her the way he was looking at her now. "Why are you doing this?" she whispered back. "I was trying so hard to get over you.''

"Please don't," her proud warrior begged. "Because I'll never get over you.''

"Then why were you kissing that woman in the bar?" she asked, desperately trying to hang on to her composure.

"Because I didn't think I was worthy of your love and I was trying to send you away for your own good. I was trying to be noble. But you were right. The guilt was eating me up. I ended up calling my dad and we talked. About Danny. It was hard, but it was the right thing to do. We worked some things out, reached some sort of closure on things.''

"I'm glad to hear that," she said in a polite voice, keeping her gaze fixed over his right shoulder.

"I still may not be worthy of you, but I love you. You take my breath away with your heart and your passion. You never gave up on me. Don't give up on me now.''

"You hurt me," she told him fiercely.

His stricken eyes met hers. "And I regret that more than I can say, Princess Pug. I'll never do it again, I swear. Marry me and I'll spend the rest of my life making it up to you.''

Hanging on to her composure was a losing battle when he was standing so close to her, his voice filled with husky tenderness, his caressing fingers brushing over her face with trembling warmth.

"What about my father?" she said brokenly, trying to step away from him. "I told him not to interfere but I can't guarantee what he'll do. I don't want him to ruin your career. I know how much the Marine Corps means to you.''

"Yes, but do you know how much *you* mean to me?" Joe asked, brushing his thumb over her lips.

Shaking her head, she stepped away from him. "I'm not going to be the reason you get tossed out of the Marines. You might want to marry me now, but you'd end up resenting me.''

"What if I told you that your father wants me to marry you?" Joe told her about his conversation with her dad. "Where are you going?" he demanded, reaching out to take her hand.

"To give him a piece of my mind. I can't believe he was matchmaking when he picked you to accompany me into the mountains. He never said a word to me.''

"You haven't answered my question yet," Joe reminded her. "Will you marry me?" When she hesitated, he said, "What happened to the Prudence willing to take a leap of faith? My own bungee-jumping days are over. The only thing I want to prove is my love for you.''

Looking into his eyes, she saw a difference there. Or was it only wishful thinking? ''I'm afraid to believe you,'' she admitted with a sob.

''And I'm afraid you'll say no, that you want no part of a life with this Marine, that you don't love me,'' he replied, hiding nothing, exposing his soul to her, letting her see his ragged doubts and fears, letting her see his passionate love and need for her in his eyes. ''But a pretty smart guy recently told me that courage isn't the absence of fear, it's overcoming fear.'' He held out his hand to her, inviting her into his arms. ''So will you overcome your fear and marry me?''

Will you? she asked herself. Will you let yourself open to that kind of pain again? Will you trust him not to hurt you again. Or will you go back into your cocoon where it's nice and safe...and lonely. In the end it wasn't that difficult a decision after all. How appropriate that she make it here, where she'd taken her first leap of faith.

''Unless you don't love me anymore?''

''Of course I love you, you idiot!'' she joyously replied, throwing herself into his arms. ''And yes, I'll marry you,'' she added as he folded her to him, molding her to his body in an exquisite fit.

''Thank you, ma'am,'' Joe murmured against her lips before kissing her with all his heart and soul.

Epilogue

Three months later....

"So, Wilder, I hear you've stopped jumping off bridges and are getting married this weekend," Sergeant Major Martin said.

"That's affirmative, sir."

"Stop picking on your future son-in-law," Ellen Martin scolded her husband. "Or I'll tell him about the mysteriously fast recovery of a certain Sergeant Brown from a supposedly ruptured appendix."

Joe didn't have time to ask what that comment might mean. Besides, he wasn't sure he really wanted to know. He just wanted everything to go right today. They were all standing around in the church foyer, waiting for the proceedings to begin. Ellen had just joined them from the top-secret bridal area to inform them that this special op otherwise known as a wedding was just about ready to commence. D-Day H-Hour rapidly approaching, in military terms.

"The church is filled with devil dog Marines," Joe's dad announced happily before adding, "but I'm not sure where all the short civilians came from."

"They're kids, Dad," Joe replied.

"Prudence invited her sixth-grade class to the wedding," Joe's mom reminded her husband.

As if on cue, Keishon showed up, wearing a dress instead of her usual message-bearing T-shirt and jeans. Rosa, Sinatra, Gem and Pete were with her. "We've got all the birdseed packets ready."

"Birdseed?" Joe's dad said in confusion.

"To throw afterward instead of rice," Keishon replied. "Uncooked rice is harmful to birds."

"And we don't want to harm the birds, right Keishon?" Joe noted.

"Right, sir. And you want to stop beating up on evergreen branches, too."

"I'll do that, Keishon," Joe said with a grin. "You guys all better go take your seats now."

"Time to synchronize your watches, gentlemen," Sergeant Major Martin said. "I've got 1400 hours right...now."

"Hey bro, is this the right place?" Joe's brother Mark inquired as he strolled through the church's front door. Taller than Joe and sharing his blue eyes, the two brothers were both wearing dress blue uniforms, as were all the Marines in attendance. "Am I late?"

"Yeah, you are," Joe growled. "I expected better from the only commissioned officer in the family."

"Well, I'm here now so let the festivities begin," Mark said, straightening Joe's collar with a teasing grin.

"Keep your mitts to yourself," Joe said in exasperation.

"Boys, boys," their father said with a shake of his head. "Not now."

"Yeah, Wilder, not now," Curt said. "I'm not standing in front of all these people as your best man while you stand out here arm wrestling your brother like you were kids. Get your rear in gear, buddy. Trust me, brides don't like you messing up their schedule."

"There are more participants than audience members," Joe muttered once they reached the front of the church and turned to watch the proceedings.

First came his parents, joining his younger brother Sam waiting in the pew. His older brother Justice wasn't able to get away from active duty but had sent his greetings and a stripper to Joe's bachelor party last night.

Once Prudence's mom was seated, the organist changed the music and Blue came floating down the aisle, tossing rose petals just as she had at Curt's wedding.

"That kid's gonna grow up to be one heck of a pitcher," Curt whispered proudly.

Next came Jessie, her eyes meeting Curt's with love. Then came...

"Who's the princess?" Mark inquired from beside him.

"Her Royal Highness Vanessa Volzemburg so be on your best behavior, damn it," Joe growled.

Then the music changed again and Joe saw Prudence. She looked like all his dreams come true. Her white dress billowed around her ankles as she walked beside her father down the aisle.

She took his breath away. He took her breath away. Prudence fixed her gaze on Joe's face. He looked so handsome, so sexy, so...*hers.* All hers! She grinned at him and he grinned back.

The ceremony was a short one, but it seemed forever until the minister declared them to be husband and wife.

''Welcome to married life, ma'am,'' Joe murmured against her lips before taking her in his arms and kissing her.

Honor, courage, commitment. Her Marine had now added love to that list of Corps values, and she was forever safe in his embrace.

* * * * *